Cami

Senso
(and other stories)

Translated from the Italian
by Christine Donougher

With an Introduction
by Roderick Conway Morris

Dedalus / Hippocrene

Published in the UK by Dedalus Limited, Langford Lodge, St Judith's Lane, Sawtry, Cambs, PE17 5XE

UK ISBN 0 946626 83 9

Published in the US by Hippocrene Books Inc, 171, Madison Avenue, New York NY10016

US ISBN 07818 0005 6

Distributed in Canada by Marginal Distribution, Unit 103, 277 George Street North, Peterborough, Ontario, KJ9 3G9

Distributed in Australia and New Zealand by Peribo Pty Ltd, 26, Tepko Road, Terrey Hills, N.S.W.2084

Publishing History
First published in Italy 1867/95
First English edition 1993

Translation copyright © Christine Donougher 1993
Introduction copyright © Dedalus 1993

Typeset by Datix International Limited, Bungay, Suffolk
Printed in England by Loader Jackson, Arlesey, Beds

This book is sold subject to the condition that it shall not, by way of trade or otherwise, be lent, resold, hired out, or otherwise circulated without the publisher's prior consent in any form of binding or cover other than that in which it is published and without a similar condition including this condition being imposed on the subsequent purchaser.

A C.I.P. listing for this title is available on request.

Contents

INTRODUCTION

by Roderick Conway Morris

I

'I have often been spoken of as decadent,' said Luchino Visconti. 'But I have a very high opinion of decadence, just as Thomas Mann did, for example. I am imbued with its spirit . . . What has always interested me is to analyse a sick society.'

Hardly surprising, therefore, that Visconti should have fallen under the spell of the Contessa Livia, the literal *femme fatale* of Camillo Boito's 'Senso', that paradigm of cruel voluptuousness, self-absorption and wanton depravity, who, by the end of the story has coolly engineered the destruction of five men (four of whom she has never even met) purely to assuage her slighted *amour propre* – emerging 'serene in the self-respect that came from having fulfilled a difficult duty.'

But then Livia's *amour propre* is not so much a character defect as the driving force behind her entire personality. Like Conrad's Nostromo, Livia is the possessor of 'enormous vanity, that finest form of egoism which can take on the aspect of every virtue', and like Wilde's Dorian Gray, the flawless exterior hides a dismal sump of internal baseness. Her vanity is indeed a source of almost onanistic pleasure:

'In Venice, I was reborn. My beauty came into full bloom. Men's eyes would light up with a gleam of desire whenever they looked at me. Even without seeing them looking, I could feel their burning gaze on my body. The women, too, would openly stare at me, then admiringly examine me from head to toe. I would smile like a queen, like a goddess. In the gratification of my vanity, I became

5

kind, indulgent, natural, carefree, witty: the greatness of my triumph made me appear almost modest.'

Visconti's 'Senso' was released in 1954, won no prizes at the Venice Film Festival (possibly because of pressure from Italy's Christian Democrat government, which found the film unpatriotic), was a considerable success with the public, and, in due course, was followed by two other captivating depictions of 19th-century Italy – based on Tomasi di Lampedusa's *Il Gattopardo* (1961) and Gabriele D'Annunzio's *L'Innocente* (1975).

Visconti considered changing the name 'Senso' – which embraces implications of sense, sensation and sensuality – but finally stuck to Boito's original title. The director's first choices for the Contessa Livia and the handsome, cowardly and degenerate Austrian officer she takes as a lover whilst on her honeymoon in Venice were Ingrid Bergman and Marlon Brando. Bergman declined and Brando was rejected by the producers after a screen test in Rome. Farley Granger was then cast as the lover, and brought a suitably creepy pusillanimity to the part. The Italian actress Alida Valli played the Contessa with verve, style and subtlety. And yet, though this is one of a great director's greatest films, which explores facets of Boito's story only touched upon in the original text, there is a dimension missing that ultimately confirms the masterly quality of Boito's first-person narrative on the page. For in the celluloid version we are deprived of the singular experience of seeing events as they unfold through Livia's own eyes, and are denied entry to the narcissistic, hair-raising hall of mirrors that is her mind – as readers of this extraordinary *tour de force* will discover for themselves.

II

Camillo Boito was born on 30 October 1836. His mother was a Polish countess, Giuseppina Radolinska, his father Silvestro an adept but never outstandingly successful painter of portraits and miniatures. Silvestro came from Polpet, a mountain village near Belluno, in the Dolomites to the north of Venice, on the banks of the river Piave. At the time, indeed until the 1930s, when the Piave's course was interrupted by dams for irrigation and hydro-electricity, the principal occupation of the riverside villages in this area was the felling and cutting of timber, built into rafts to convey the wood to Venice for the construction of buildings, ships and boats. Hundreds of rafts made the journey every year, and guiding them through the river's shifting shoals and rapids was a skilful and perilous task. The immediacy with which Boito wrote about the hardships of life and evoked the majestic beauty of mountain landscapes is reflected in two of the stories translated here. 'Vade Retro, Satana' is set in a poor village in the Trentino, and opens with a wonderfully observed description of a spectacular storm boiling in the valley below. 'The Grey Blotch' takes place among the peaks to the west of Lake Garda, and contains a daring extended description of a rushing river – in which it may not be fanciful to detect an echo of that centuries-old battle the rafters of his grandparents' village fought with the treacherous waters of the Piave to wrest a livelihood from the river.

After leaving Polpet at the age of eighteen to seek his fortune as a painter, Silvestro embarked on a peripatetic life in search of commissions, spending time in Padua, Venice, and Vienna, wandering as far as St Petersburg. On one of these journeys he met Giuseppina Radolinska. Not least of her attractions was her fairly substantial means, and the formalization of their relationship was no doubt hastened by her pregnancy – Camillo being born in Rome less than five months after the couple's marriage in Florence.

After some success at winning the patronage of Pope Gregory XVI, who also came from the Belluno region and whose portrait Silvestro painted more than once, the Boito couple resumed their travels. Camillo's younger brother Arrigo was born in Padua in February 1842.

The family then settled in Venice, where in 1848–9, during the short-lived revival of the Venetian Republic, Silvestro fought alongside the revolutionaries. By 1851 Giuseppina's fortune had been exhausted, the marriage had broken down, and she had gone back to Poland. Silvestro, who lived apart from his sons after this, died in 1856, leaving the family more or less destitute. Meanwhile, Giuseppina returned to Milan to be with Arrigo, before dying in 1859.

Despite the vicissitudes of their early life, both Camillo and Arrigo received a good education, the lack of a stable domestic background being compensated for by the interest shown in them by family friends, who did much to nurture their clearly exceptional intellectual and artistic talents. Camillo found a dedicated mentor in the art historian Pietro Selvatico. After studying under him at the Accademia di Belle Arti in Venice, Camillo succeeded Selvatico as Professor of Architecture at the Accademia at the remarkable age of nineteen. Arrigo went to study violin, piano and composition at the Conservatory in Milan. In 1860 Camillo joined his brother in Lombardy, having been appointed Professor of Architecture at Milan's Accademia di Brera, a prestigious post he was to occupy continuously until 1909. The move was a timely one, since by then Camillo was under imminent threat of arrest by the Austrians, who ruled Venice until 1866.

When Camillo arrived in Milan, Arrigo's studies were drawing to a close and he was preparing to launch himself on his career as a poet and composer, which would eventually lead to the collaboration with Giuseppe Verdi (1813–1901) as the librettist of *Otello* and *Falstaff* that won him lasting fame.

The Boito brothers remained intellectually and emotionally close throughout their lives, and shared the same house in Milan after Camillo's second wife died, until his own death on 28 June 1914. The tenderness of this fraternal bond, strengthened no doubt by the travails of their younger days, is well caught in a letter by Camillo to

Arrigo, written in April 1862: 'You know how much I love you, and how every honour and every eulogy you receive brings me greater comfort, greater indeed than if I were receiving them myself.'

Camillo Boito's professional life was devoted almost entirely to the practice and teaching of architecture and the study of architectural history. His first major·commission on reaching Milan was the restoration of the city's 12th-century Porta Ticinese. Numerous other works of restoration followed on palazzi and churches in Milan, Padua and Venice. He became a noted theorist on the principals of restoration, and was one of the first to advocate more sensitive and less interventionist approaches (though he seems not always to have put his own arguments into practice). His original designs included schools, hospitals, the Verdi Musicians' Home in Milan, sepulchral monuments and the bronze doors of the Basilica of St Antony in Padua. His writings on Italian medieval architecture – out of which he sought to create a new style for modern Italy – were particularly influential. He was also one of the first Italian scholars to take a special interest in minor and applied arts and industrial architecture.

III

It may seem surprising that such a mainstream academic figure as Boito should have taken to writing fantastic, bizarre and often risqué tales peopled by an assortment of odd-balls, misfits and perverts. But Boito, having grown up during the Risorgimento – Italy's forty-year-long struggle for unification and self-determination, with its countless setbacks and disappointments - was perhaps not unlike many of his contemporaries who felt a strong sense of disillusionment at its outcome and continued to dream of a more radical transformation of Italian art and society.

One of the primary manifestations of this unabated revolutionary tendency was beginning to flower in Milan at the very time that Boito arrived there from Venice. Dubbed the *Scapigliatura* (from *scapigliato*, meaning 'dishevelled, unkempt, loose-living, profligate'), this was partly inspired by French bohemianism and earlier Romantic rebels. Its proponents were anti the bougeoisie, the Church, the Establishment, and tradition, and pro individualism, hedonism, sexual freedom, drunkenness and general degeneracy. They argued for the superiority of the unruly, unfettered artist over the wealthy, privileged and conventional. Among the principal *scapigliati* were the writers Carlo Righetti (who invented the term), Giuseppe Rovani, Igino Ugo Tarchetti, Carlo Dossi, and the poet-painters Emilio Praga and Giovanni Camerana. Praga and Tarchetti lived out the movement's manifesto to the letter, dying prematurely of drink and syphilis, and Camerana killed himself.

Arrigo Boito fully aligned himself with the *Scapigliatura*, and became one of its leading lights, writing poetry about ghosts, graveyards, ruined castles, a mummy waiting to burst out of a glass case, light and darkness, dualistic angst, and other subjects dear to the movement. In 1863 Arrigo published 'All'Arte Italiana' (To Italian Art), subtitled 'A Sapphic Ode with Glass in Hand', in which he drinks to the health of Italian art, newly liberated from 'the blindness of the old and the cretinous', whom he excoriates for having besmirched the altar of art 'like the wall of a brothel.' Unhappily, Giuseppe Verdi interpreted the verses as including himself among the geriatric vandals, and subsequently resolutely refused to work with Arrigo – thus postponing for two decades what turned out to be such a fruitful partnership.

It was against the backdrop of the *Scapigliatura*'s most active period that, in 1867, Camillo Boito began to write his novellas and short stories. Yet Boito never seems to have considered himself a card-carrying member of the movement, as it were, nor to have been thought of as such by his contemporaries, and to try to force his work into that mould would be to ignore its distinctive qualities.

10

Three stories, nonetheless, included in this selection do have *scapigliatura* flavours. 'Christmas Eve' relates how a brother's incestuous passion for his saintly dead twin sister leads to his infatuation with a coarse shop-girl who resembles her. 'The Grey Blotch' is about a man tormented by an inexplicable patch in his vision, after he has seduced and debauched a country girl, only to desert her, repelled by her voracious sexual appetite and feral physicality.

The novella 'A Body', first published in a periodical in 1870, is especially interesting in that his brother, Arrigo, based a poem (written in 1865, but not published until 1874) on a similar scenario, and revolving around some of the same questions of the conflict between art and science. Arrigo's 'Lezione D'Anatomia' (An Anatomy Lesson) is set in a chilly morgue, where the corpse of a consumptive young girl is to be dissected:

> *Ed era giovane!*
> *Ed era bionda!*
> *Ed era bella!*

(And she was young!/And she was blonde!/And she was beautiful!)

As the dissection proceeds the observer falls into a reverie as he imagines the girl in life, recoiling from the pathologist's booming voice and brutal exposure of her internal organs.

> *Scienza, vattene*
> *Co' tuoi conforti!*
> *Ridammi i mondi*
> *Del sogno e l'anima!*
> *Sia pace ai morti*
> *E ai moribondi.*

(Science, be off/with your proofs!/Give back to me the world/of dreams, of the spirit!/Peace be to the dead,/and to the dying.)

★

11

Characteristically, the verses end with a twist, when the poet's 'pious, sweet, purest' of virgins is revealed to have in her womb the month-old foetus of a child.

Camillo Boito's 'The Body' is a tale full of suspense set against the gay, heady bohemianism of Vienna's pleasure gardens in spring. A brilliant new artist is engaged in immortalizing his exquisitely lovely and vivacious mistress on canvas, whilst the ambitious and sinister young anatomist Professor Gulz (whose limitless faith in the primacy of science chillingly presages the demonic monomania of Hitler's medical establishment) shadows her, convinced that she will soon yield up the true mysteries of her beauty beneath his scalpel on the mortuary slab.

The medical profession appears again in 'Buddha's Collar', the final story of the present selection. This macabre but comic tale is of a timid and naive Venetian bank clerk, who becomes entangled with a pretty young prostitute. After being bitten by the girl, he is consumed by the fear that he might contract rabies, and is unlucky to find himself the centre of an animated debate in the backroom of a pharmacy, where some off-duty medics are passing the time. The young man is far from comforted by the view of a senior practitioner, in whom long experience has bred a humane humility alien to the fanatical certainties of Professor Gulz: 'The conclusion to be drawn is this,' said the old doctor. 'That we know nothing about it.'

All of Boito's seventeen novellas and stories were written between 1867 and 1895, and most were initially published in periodicals. When they appeared in book form, they were well received critically, the lucidity of the author's style, the vividness of his descriptive powers and the liveliness of his imagination being generally praised. Boito also proved popular with the public. The first volume, *Storielle Vane* (Vain Tales), published in Milan in 1876, went through seven editions by 1895. The second, *Senso: Nuove Storielle Vane* (Senso: New Vain Tales), brought out in 1883, was reprinted five times by 1899.

We may only regret, along with the critic Navarro della

Miraglia reviewing *Storielle Vane* in the literary journal *Fanfulla*, that the author did not produce more of his strange and engaging tales: 'I read them with eagerness and pleasure. I do not know why the author of this book writes so rarely and so little. He has all the qualities needed to be in the front rank of that little vanguard of our writers of fiction. He has the imagination, clarity, colour. He has the simplicity and truth of expression, those two supreme merits that bring things to life.'

A Bibliographical Note

'The Body' ('*Il Corpo*') and 'Christmas Eve' ('*Notte di Natale*') are translated from *Storielle Vane* (Milan, 1913); 'Senso', 'Vade Retro, Satana', 'The Grey Blotch' ('*Macchia Grigia*') and 'Buddha's Collar' ('*Il Collare di Budda*') from *Senso: Nuove Storielle Vane* (Milan, 1883). The most readily available Italian edition of the stories is presently *Senso: Storielle Vane* (edited with an introduction and bibliography by Raffaella Bertazzoli), published in paperback by Garzanti (Milan, 1990).

SENSO

FROM CONTESSA LIVIA'S SECRET NOTEBOOK

Yesterday in my yellow drawing-room, the young lawyer Gino, his voice thick with long-repressed passion, was whispering in my ear, 'Contessa, take pity on me. Drive me away, instruct the servants not to let me in any more, but in God's name release me from this deadly uncertainty. Tell me whether there's any hope for me, or not . . . ' The poor boy threw himself at my feet, while I stood there, unperturbed, looking at myself in the mirror.

I was examining my face in search of a wrinkle. My forehead, framed with pretty little curls, is smooth and clear as a baby's. There is not a line to be seen on either side of my flared nostrils, or above my rather full, red lips. I have never found a single white strand in my long hair, which, when loose, falls in lovely glossy waves, blacker than ink, over my snow-white shoulders.

Thirty-nine! I shudder as I write this horrible figure.

I gave a light slap with my tapering fingers to the hot hand groping towards me, and was on my way out of the room. I do not know what prompted me – surely some laudable sense of compassion or friendship – but on the threshold I turned and whispered, I think, these words: 'There's hope . . . '

I must curb my vanity. The anxiety that gnaws at my mind, leaving virtually no trace on my body, alternates with overconfidence in my beauty, leaving me no other comfort but this: my mirror.

I hope to find further comfort in writing of what happened to me sixteen years ago, an experience I look back on with bitter delight. This notebook, which I keep triple-locked in my secret safe, away from all prying eyes, and as soon as I have reached the end of my story I shall throw it on the fire, dispersing the ashes, but confiding my old memories to paper should help to abate their persistently caustic edge. Every word and deed, and above all every humiliation, of that feverish period in my past remains etched in my mind. And I am always testing and probing the lesions of this unhealed wound, not really knowing whether what I feel is actually pain or an itch of pleasure.

What a joy it is, to confide in no one but yourself, free from scruples, hypocrisy and reserve, respecting the truth in your recollections, even with regard to what ridiculous social conventions make it most difficult to speak of publicly: the depths to which you have sunk! I have read of holy anchorites who lived in the midst of vermin and putrefaction (filth, that is), but who believed that the more they wallowed in the mire, the higher they elevated themselves. So my spirit exalts in self-humiliation. I take pride in the sense of being utterly different from other women. There is no sight whatsoever that daunts me. There is, in my weakness, a daring strength: I am like the women of ancient Rome who gave the thumbs-down, those women that Parini mentions in one of his odes – I don't remember it exactly, but I know that when I read it I really thought that the poet could have been referring to me.

Were it not for the feverishness of vivid memories on the one hand and dread of old age on the other, I should be a happy woman. My husband, who is old and infirm, and utterly dependent on me, allows me to spend as much as I want and to do as I please. I am one of the first ladies of Trento. I have no lack of admirers, and, far from lessening, the kind envy of my dear women friends is ever mounting.

I was of course more beautiful at the age of twenty. Not that my features have changed, or that my body seems any less slender and supple, but there was in my eyes a flame, which now, alas, is dying. The very blackness of my pupils seems to me on close inspection a little less intense. They say that the purpose of philosophy is to know yourself. I have studied myself with so much trepidation for so many years, hour by hour, minute by minute, that I believe I know myself through and through, and can declare myself an excellent philosopher.

I would say that I was at my most beautiful (there is always in a woman's blossoming a brief period of consummate loveliness), when I had just turned twenty-two, in Venice. It was July of the year 1865. I had been married for only a few days and was on my honeymoon. For my husband, who could have been my grandfather, I felt indifference mingled with pity and contempt. He bore his sixty-two years and his ample paunch with seeming vigour. He dyed his sparse hair and thick moustaches with a rank ointment that stained his pillows with big yellowish blotches. Otherwise, he was an amiable man, in his own way full of attentions for his young wife, inclined to gluttony, an occasional blasphemer, an indefatigable smoker, a haughty aristocrat, a bully towards the meek and himself timorous in the face of aggression, a lively raconteur of lewd stories that he would tell at every opportunity, neither tight-fisted nor a spendthrift. He would strut like a peacock when holding me on his arm, yet eyed with a smile of lascivious connivance the women of easy virtue who passed us in Piazza San Marco. And from one point of view I was pleased by this, since I would happily have banished him into the arms of any other woman, just to be rid of him; and from another, it vexed me.

I had taken him of my own free will. Indeed, I had actually wanted him. My family were opposed to so ill-assorted a match. Nor, if truth be told, was the poor man ardently seeking my hand. But I was bored with my position as an unmarried woman. I wanted to have my own carriages, jewels, velvet gowns, a title, and above all my freedom. It took a few flirtatious glances to inflame the desire of the pot-bellied Count, but once inflamed, he could not rest until I was his, neither did he mind about the small dowry, nor give any thought to the future. Before the priest, I answered with a firm and resounding 'I do'. I was pleased with what I had done, and I do not regret it now, after all these years. Even in those days, when I suddenly lost my heart and surrendered myself to the frenzy of a first blind passion, I did not really think I had anything to regret. Until the age of twenty-two, my heart had remained impervious. My women friends, who weakened when confronted with the allurements of romantic love, envied and respected me. To them, my coolness, in my disdainful indifference to fond words and languishing glances showed common sense and strength of character. I had already established my reputation at sixteen, by trifling with the affections of a good-looking young fellow from my home town, and then afterwards spurning him, with the result that the poor boy tried to kill himself. And when he had recovered, he left Trento and ran away to Piedmont to join up as a volunteer. He died in one of the battles of '59 – I don't remember which. I was too young then to feel any remorse. And besides, my parents, relatives and acquaintances, all of them devoted to the Austrian government, which they served loyally as soldiers and administrators, had nothing else to say about the young hot-head's death but, 'Serves him right!'

In Venice, I was reborn. My beauty came into full bloom. Men's eyes would light up with a gleam of desire whenever they looked at me. Even without seeing them looking, I could feel their burning gaze on my body. The women, too, would openly stare at me, then admiringly examine me from head to toe. I would smile like a queen, like a goddess. In the gratification of my vanity, I became kind, indulgent, natural, carefree, witty: the greatness of my triumph made me appear almost modest.

I was invited with my husband, a representative of the Tyrolese nobility at the Diet of Innsbruck, to the Imperial Lord-Lieutenant's dinners and soirées. Whenever I entered a room, with my arms bare, in a *décolleté* gown of velvet and lace with a very long train, wearing a great flower of rubies with leaves of emeralds in my hair, I would sense a murmur running all around me. A blush of satisfaction would colour my cheeks. I would unassumingly take a few slow, solemn steps, without looking at anybody, and as the hostess came towards me and invited me to sit next to her, I would wave my fan in front of my face as if to hide modestly from the eyes of the astonished guests.

I never missed an occasion for a gondola-ride on the Grand Canal, in the cool of a summer's evening, when serenades were sung. At Quadri's café in Piazza San Marco I was surrounded by a host of satellites, as if I were the sun of a new planetary system. I would laugh, mock and tease those who tried to win me with their sighs or verses. I gave the impression of being an impregnable fortress, yet I did not try too hard to appear truly impregnable lest I discouraged anyone. My court of admirers consisted largely of junior officers and Tyrolese officials who were rather dull and very self-satisfied, which meant that the most fun were the most irresponsible; those who from their dissolute life had acquired, if nothing else, the insolent boldness of their own follies. There was one I knew who stood out from the crowd for two reasons. According to his own friends, he combined reckless profligacy with such a cynical lack of moral principles that nothing in this world seemed to him worthy of respect, save the penal code and military regulations. Besides which, he really was extremely handsome and extraordinarily strong: a cross between Adonis and Alcides. His complexion was white and rosy, he had blond curly hair, a beardless chin, ears so small they were like a girl's, and big restless-looking eyes of sky-blue. The expression on his face was sometimes mild, and sometimes fierce, but of a fierceness and mildness tempered by signs of a constant, almost cruel, irony. His head was set magnificently on his sturdy neck. His shoulders were not square and heavy, but sloped down gracefully. A close-fitting, white uniform of an Austrian officer showed off to perfection his muscular physique, which brought to mind those Roman statues of gladiators.

This infantry lieutenant, who was only twenty-four, two years older than me, had already succeeded in squandering the large estate inherited from his father, and still he continued to gamble, and whore, and to live like a lord – nobody could understand how he managed it. Yet no one excelled him in swimming, gymnastics, or physical strength. He had never had occasion to take part in battle, and he did not care for duelling. In fact, two young officers told me one evening that rather than fight, he had more than once swallowed the most appalling insults. Strong, handsome, degenerate, reprobate – I was attracted by him. I did not let him know it, because I took delight in teasing and riling this latter-day Hercules.

Venice, which I had never seen and so longed to see, spoke more to my senses than my intellect: I cared less for its monuments, whose history I did not know and beauty I did not understand, than for its green waters, starry skies, silvery moon, golden sunsets, and above all the black gondola in which I would recline, abandoning myself to the most voluptuous caprices of my imagination. In the intense heat of July, after a blazing-hot day, the fresh breeze would caress my brow as I travelled by boat from the Piazzetta to the island of Sant'Elena, or beyond, to Sant'Elisabetta and San Nicolo on the Lido: that west wind impregnated with a sharp salty tang would revive my limbs and my spirits, and seemed to whisper in my ears the passionate secrets of true love. I would trail my bare arm up to the elbow in the water, letting the lace trim on my short sleeve get wet; and then I watched the drops of water falling from my fingernails one by one, like the purest diamonds. One evening I took a ring from my finger – a ring my husband had given me, set with a big sparkling solitaire – and threw it far from the boat into the lagoon: I felt I had married the sea.

One day the Lord-Lieutenant's wife insisted on taking me to see the Accademia Gallery: I understood next to nothing. Since then, from travelling, and from talking to artists (there was one, as handsome as Raphael, who desperately wanted to teach me to paint), I have learned a few things; but at the time, although I did not know anything, the brightness of those colours, the richness of those reds, yellows, greens, blues, and whites – like painted music, rendered with such sensual passion – seemed to me not art but a Venetian aspect of Nature. And in the presence of Titian's golden *Assumption*, Paolo Veronese's magnificent *Feast*, or Bonifazio's fleshy, carnal, gleaming faces, I would be put in mind of the uninhibited songs I had heard the common people singing.

My husband smoked, snored, spoke ill of Piedmont, and bought himself cosmetics; I needed someone to love.

Now, this is how my terrible passion began for the Alcides, the white-uniformed Adonis with a name not much to my liking: Remigio. I was in the habit of going to Rima's floating baths, situated between the gardens of the Royal Palace and the Customs House Point. I had hired for one hour, from seven till eight, the Sirena, one of the two women's baths big enough to swim around in a little, and my maid came along to undress and dress me. But since no one else could enter, I did not bother to put on bathing clothes. The bath was screened round with wooden panels and covered with a grey awning with broad red stripes. The slated bottom was fixed at a depth to allow women of small stature to stand with their heads above the water, which did not even cover my shoulders.

O that lovely, clear, emerald-green water, in which I could see the shape of my body gracefully undulating, right down to my slender feet! And a few tiny, silvery fish darted around me. I swam the length of the Sirena; I beat the water with the flat of my hand until that diaphanous green was covered with white spray; I lay on my back, letting my long hair soak in the water, and trying to keep afloat for a moment without moving; I splashed my maid, who ran away; I laughed like a child.

A number of large openings, just below the surface, let the water flow in and out freely, and if you put your eye to the gaps in the ill-fitted screens you could see something of what was outside: the red campanile of San Giorgio, a stretch of the lagoon with boats swiftly sailing past, a thin strip of the military baths floating a little way off from my Sirena.

I knew that Lieutenant Remigio went swimming there. He cut such an heroic figure in the water: he would dive in head first, pick up a bottle from the bottom, and emerge from the bathing area by swimming out underneath the dressing rooms. I found his strength and agility so alluring, I would have given anything to be able to see him.

One morning while I was examining a bluish mark on my right thigh, probably a slight bruise, which marred a little the rosy whiteness of my skin, I heard a noise outside that sounded like someone swimming very fast. The disturbance of the water made cool waves that sent a shiver down my limbs, and all of a sudden, through one of the large gaps between the bottom of the pool and the screens, a man came into the Sirena. I did not cry out; I was not afraid. He was so white and handsome, he looked as if he were made of marble, but his broad chest rose and fell as he took deep breaths, and his blue eyes shone, and drops of water fell from his fair hair like a shower of lustrous pearls. He stood upright, half covered by the still unsettled water, and raised his limber, muscular arms aloft; he seemed to be rendering thanks to the gods, and saying, 'At last!'

So began our relationship. And from then on I saw him every day, whether out for a walk, or at a café or restaurant – for my husband had taken a liking to him, and often invited him. I also saw him in secret, and gradually our clandestine meetings became a positively daily occurrence. We were often alone for one or two hours, while the count slept between luncheon and dinner or went wandering off on his own round the city; then we would spend two or three hours together in public, exchanging the occasional fleeting handclasp. Sometimes he would step on my foot, often hurting me so much I became quite red in the face, but this very pain gave me pleasure. Never had I looked so beautiful, to others and to myself, never so healthy and light-hearted and happy – with myself, with life, with everything and everybody. The wicker chair that I sat on in Piazza San Marco became a throne. I thought that the military band that played Strauss waltzes and Meyerbeer melodies in front of the Old Procurators' Building were performing their music solely for me, and the blue sky and ancient monuments seemed to rejoice in my happiness.

Our meeting-place was not always the same. Sometimes Remigio would be waiting for me in a closed gondola on the filthy quayside of some long, dark alley leading to a narrow canal, lined with poor houses so decrepit and crooked they looked as if they were falling down, with rags of every colour hanging from the windows. And there were other times when, throwing caution to the winds, we would take a boat in some busy part of the city, even from the landing in front of the Piazzetta. Wearing a thick veil to cover my face, I would visit him in a house by the barracks at San Sepolcro, encountering in the dark shadows of its winding staircase officers and men who would not let me pass without some show of gallantry. In that house, where the sun never shone, the musty smell of dampness was combined with the nauseating stench of stale tobacco smoke hanging in the air in those unventilated rooms.

This young lawyer Gino irritates me. He looks at me with those wildly staring eyes that often make me laugh, but sometimes make my blood run cold. He says he cannot go on living without some kind word of affection from me; he begs, weeps, sobs. He keeps saying, 'Contessa, do you remember that day when you turned to me, there in the doorway, and said in the voice of an angel, "There's hope for you."' And he goes on and on, begging for pity, sobbing and weeping. I cannot stand any more of it. A few days ago I let him take my hand. He kissed it repeatedly, so hard that he left bruises on my skin. The fact is, I am tired of him! Yesterday I lost my temper. I shouted at him,

25

and told him not to bother me any more, and said that he was never to attempt to set foot in my house again, and if he ever dared to show his face I would have him thrown out by the servants, and would tell the count the whole story. He turned so pale that his black eyes looked like two holes in a wall of plaster. He rose from the sofa and staggered out, without looking at me. He'll be back, he'll be back, I bet he will. But the sad truth is, the only thing capable of affecting me deeply is the memory of a man of whose total degeneracy I was, to the shame of raging passion for him, perfectly aware.

Every so often Remigio would ask me for money. At first he did so in a roundabout way: he had some gambling debt, or there was a dinner to which he had to treat his companions for some special occasion – he would return the money in a few days' time. In the end he was asking for a hundred florins here, two hundred florins there, without any excuse. Once he asked me for a thousand lire. I gave it to him, and was pleased to give it. I had some savings of my own and, besides, my husband was generous towards me, indeed he was happy when I asked him for something. But there came a point when he thought I was spending too much. I took offence and became furiously angry; as a rule easy-going and compliant, he held out for a whole day.

That was the day that Remigio urgently needed two hundred and fifty florins, straightaway. He was so loving, and said so many sweet things, in a voice so passionate that I was glad to be able to give him a diamond hairpin, which, if I remember rightly, cost forty gold napoleons.

The next day Remigio failed to keep our appointment. I spent a good hour pacing up and down some of those little alleyways on the far side of the Rialto Bridge, causing people to eye me with sly curiosity, and prompting jokes at my expense. In the end, my cheeks were burning with shame and tears of anger filled my eyes. Despairing by then of meeting my lover, and imagining God knows what might have happened to him, I ran to his house, panting for breath and almost out of my mind.

His batman, who was polishing his sabre, told me that there had been no sight of the lieutenant since the day before.

'Out all night?' I asked, not quite understanding.

Whistling, the soldier nodded.

'For God's sake, run and find out what's happened to him. He must have had some dreadful accident – he may have been injured, or killed!'

The soldier shrugged, with a sarcastic laugh.

'Well, tell me, where is the lieutenant?' As he continued to laugh, I had grabbed the soldier by the arm, and I shook him hard. He brought his moustache right up close to my face. I leapt back, but said again, 'For pity's sake, tell me.'

He finally growled, 'Dining with Gigia, or Cate, or Nana, or with all three together. A dreadful accident? Hah!'

I realized then that Lieutenant Remigio was my life. My blood froze. I collapsed almost unconscious on the bed in that dingy room, and had he not at that moment appeared in the doorway my heart would have burst in a fit of rage and suspicion. I was insanely jealous; if need be, I was capable of becoming criminally jealous.

It was the very depravity of the man that attracted me.

When he declared, 'I swear to you, Livia, I shall never love or embrace any other woman but you . . . ', I believed him. And when he knelt before me, I looked at him adoringly, as though he were a god. If anyone had asked me, 'Would you have Remigio become a hero?', I would have replied no. What use would I have had for a hero? Perfect virtue would have seemed dull and worthless compared with his vices. To me, his infidelity, dishonesty, wantonness and lack of restraint constituted a mysterious but powerful strength to which I was happy, and proud, to enslave myself. The more depraved his heart appeared, the more wonderfully handsome his body.

27

Twice only, and only momentarily, I would have wished him to be different. We were walking one day along the quayside of a canal marking the perimeter of the Arsenal. It was a blindingly bright, sunny morning. On our left, the tall chimneys, their tops like upturned bells, the white cornices and red roofs stood against the turquoise-blue sky, whilst on our right, austere and forbidding, ran the long boundary wall round the shipyards. We rested our dazzled eyes upon dark patches of shade, in the gloom of an archway or narrow alley. And the water glistened with every shade of green, reflecting every colour, disappearing here and there into cavernous holes and strips of dense blackness. There were ten or twelve young urchins running and jumping along the canalside, which had no barrier of any kind on the waterfront, and shouting at the tops of their voices. Some of them were very small, some were a bit older. One of the younger ones – a tubby little fellow, practically naked, with blond curls crowning his pink, chubby face – was making a fiendish racket, cuffing and pinching his companions, then running off like streaked lightning.

I stopped to watch, while Remigio was telling me of his past extravagances. All of a sudden, in his headlong rush, that little demon of a child was unable to stop himself at the edge of the quay and went flying into the canal. There was a yell and a splash, then at once the air was ringing with the cries of all the children and all the women who had been talking in the street or looking out of their windows. But above the clamour rose the shrill, desperate, piercing shriek of the young mother, who threw herself at Remigio's feet – he being the only man on the scene – screaming, 'Save him, please, save him!'

With icy coldness Remigio said to the woman, 'I can't swim.'

Meanwhile, one of the older boys had jumped into the water, grabbed the youngster by his blond curls and dragged him to the bank. It all happened in an instant. The screeching turned into enthusiastic cheers; women and children wept with joy; people came running from all around to see; and the fair-haired child looked around with his big blue eyes, amazed at such a fuss. With a violent tug Remigio drew me away from the crowd.

The other time that my lover somewhat disappointed me, the reason was as follows. He had been overheard, at Quadri's, speaking German with some Tyrolese officials, loudly disparaging the Venetians. A gentleman sitting in a corner leapt to his feet, and planting himself in front of Remigio, who was in uniform, he shouted, 'Soldier, you're a coward!' And he threw three or four visiting cards in his face. Pandemonium broke out. The next day the seconds were supposed to arrange the duel, but having noticed that his adversary was a small thin man, and not very strong, Remigio refused pistols, and he refused swords; although the choice of weapons should have been the challenger's, being confident of the strength of his own arm, he insisted on sabres. The Venetian gave way to his high-handedness, but was imprisoned before the duel could take place, and Remigio received orders to proceed immediately to a new posting in Croatia.

When I learned of this I was in despair: I could not live without that man. I so prevailed upon the Lord-Lieutenant's wife, and my husband, at my entreaty, so lobbied the Governor and the Generals, that Remigio managed to get himself transferred to Trento, just when the count and I were due to return there. Everything thus far had favoured my blind passion.

I have not set eyes on this notebook of mine for the past three months. I dared not take it away with me, and, I confess, I regretted leaving it behind in Trento. Going back in my mind over those events of so long ago, my heartbeat starts to quicken again, and I feel the hot breath of youth blowing around me.

My manuscript has been kept under triple lock in my secret safe at the back of the alcove in my bedroom; and it was sealed, with five seals, inside a big envelope, on which

I had written in large letters, before going away, 'I entrust to my husband's honour the secret of these pages, which he is to burn without opening, after my death.'

I went away without the slightest misgiving. I was sure that, whatever his suspicions, the count would have religiously carried out his wife's wishes.

My maid has just told me something that has annoyed me: the young lawyer Gino is getting married.

So much for the faithfulness of men, so much for undying passion! 'Contessa Livia, I shall die, I shall kill myself. Not until I've shed the very last drop of my blood will your image fade from my heart. Treat me like a slave, but allow me to adore you like a goddess.' Melodramatic words, but a few months later and there is nothing left to show for them: love, frenzy, vows, tears, sobs – all gone without trace. How contemptible is human nature! And seeing those black eyes in that pallid face, anyone would have said that they gleamed with the deep sincerity of an impassioned soul. How his lips stammered and his arteries throbbed and his hands trembled and his whole body grovelled at my feet. That despicable, scrufulous wretch of a lawyer richly deserved to be sent packing. The dolt!

And whom is he marrying? An eighteen-year-old ninny whose parents would not bring her to my house because Contessa Livia is known to be too risquée. A vapid creature with two red apples for cheeks; short, fat, pink hands; a stable-boy's feet; and the pert air of a little saint, as a consolation. And the man who is taking such a goose for his wife dared to love me and to tell me so! It makes my face burn . . .

Even if he was no gentleman, that officer of mine, sixteen years ago, was at least a real man. When he put his arms around my waist, he used to squeeze the breath out of me, and he would bite my shoulders until they bled.

Vague rumours of war began to circulate, and then came the usual contradictory announcements and the usual denials: they're arming, they're not arming, yes, no. Meanwhile, a certain mood, at once feverish and mysterious, spread from the military to civilians. The trains began to run late, and to bring in more soldiers and horses and carriages and cannons, while the newspapers kept denying that there was even the slightest mobilisation going on at all. Ignoring the evidence of my own eyes, I believed the newspapers, so scared I was by the thought of a war. I feared for my lover's life; but I feared even more the long inevitable separation that it would surely have meant for us. And indeed, on the last day of March, Remigio was ordered to report to Verona. Before his departure, he was given two days' leave, which we spent together, never for one moment apart, in the shabby room of an inn on Lake Cavedine. And he swore to come and see me soon, and I swore to go to Verona if he could not get away. As I kissed him for the last time, I thrust into his pocket a purse containing fifty napoleons.

When the count returned from the country, ten or twelve days after Remigio had gone, he found me thin and pale. I really was suffering horribly. Every so often my head would start to swim and I would feel dizzy, and three or four times I was so unsteady I had to lean against the wall or a piece of furniture so as not to fall. The doctors that my husband, concerned and worried, insisted on consulting kept shrugging their shoulders and saying, 'It's a matter of nerves.' They told me to take exercise, to eat, sleep and cheer up.

It was mid April and by then the preparations for war were undisguised. All types of soldiers filled the streets; battalions marched to the sound of brass bands and drums; aides-de camp went flying past on their horses; old generals, a little bent in the saddle, rode at a trot, followed by the General Staff, looking bold and splendid on their prancing mounts. These preparations filled me with grotesque fears. The Italians wanted to kill all the Austrians; Garibaldi and his hordes of red devils wanted to butcher every prisoner taken captive: there was clearly going to be a bloodbath.

I was in a complete state of frenzy. In six weeks I had

received only four letters from Verona. The postal service was virtually non-existent: letters had to be entrusted, after much begging and bribing, to anybody willing to face the difficulties and interminable delays the journey entailed; someone who needed, and dared, to travel from one place to another. Unable any longer to bear the anguish to which Remigio's silence, whether deliberate or innocent, condemned me night and day, I had determined to attempt the journey. But how was I to manage, a beautiful young woman alone amid the brutality of soldiers made bolder by loose discipline and by the thought of the very dangers they were about to meet.

One morning at daybreak, having fallen asleep after an endless night spent tossing and turning, I was suddenly awakened by a noise. I opened my eyes and saw Remigio at my bedside. I thought I was dreaming.

The soft, rosy light of dawn already brightened the room. I leapt out of bed to close the alcove curtains, and we began to talk in lowered voices. I was worried: the count, who was sleeping in the next room but one, might hear us, and appear; the servants might have seen my lover stealing in at this early hour. He reassured me with a few impatient words: as on previous occasions he had knocked at the ground-floor window where the chambermaid slept. She had opened the door to him very quietly and he had entered without anyone having the least suspicion. I was not much bothered about the maid, since she already knew everything; but the worst part was getting out: he had to be quick. I jumped out of bed again and went to listen at the door of my husband's room: he was snoring.

'You're stopping in Trento, aren't you?'

'You've taken leave of your senses.'

'A few days at least?'

'Impossible.'

'A day?'

'I'm leaving in an hour.'

I was devastated. Brimming with bright hope the moment before, my heart was now filled with anguish and fear.

'And don't try to keep me. War is no time for playing games.'

'Damn the war!'

'You're right. By all accounts, it's going to be terrible.'

'Listen, couldn't you run away, couldn't you hide? I'll help you. I don't want your life to be in danger.'

'Don't be silly. I'd be found and captured, and shot as a deserter.'

'Shot!'

'There's something I need from you.'

'My life, anything.'

'No, two thousand five hundred florins.'

'My God, how am I to manage that?'

'Do you want to save me?'

'At whatever the price.'

'Then listen. For two thousand five hundred florins two doctors from the military hospital and two with the brigade will issue me with a genuine sickness certificate, and come and visit me occasionally in order to confirm to HQ that I have some complaint which makes me totally unfit for service. I don't lose rank, I don't lose any pay, I'm out of any danger, able to stay quietly at home, limping a little, it's true, because of a bad attack of sciatica or a damaged leg-bone, but safe and happy. I'll find some petty clerk to play cards with; I'll eat and drink and sleep in late. It will be a bore having to be at home all day, but at night, still taking care to limp slightly, I'll be able to get out and have some fun. How do you like that?'

'I'd like it, if you were in Trento. I'd see you every day, twice a day. Once they believe you're ill, it's all the same whether you're in Verona or Trento, isn't it?'

'No, the regulations are that a sick soldier has to remain where Headquarters are based, under the doctors' constant and scrupulous supervision. But I shall return as soon as the war is over – the fighting will be bitter, but brief.'

'Will you love me always, will you always be faithful, will you never look at another woman? Do you swear?'

'Yes, yes, I swear. But it's getting late and I need those two thousand five hundred florins.'

'Right away?'

'Of course. I must take them with me.'

'But I doubt that there are even fifty gold napoleons in my safe. I never keep much money.'

'Well, find some.'

'What do you mean, find some? How do you expect me to ask my husband, now, at this hour – with what excuse, to give to whom?'

'The proof of love is making sacrifices. You don't love me then.'

'Not love you? When I'd willingly give you every drop of my blood.'

'That's just talk. If you haven't the money, give me jewellery.'

I did not answer, and felt myself turn pale.

Realizing the effect his last words had had upon me, Remigio clasped me in his arms of iron, and in a different tone of voice repeated several times, 'You know I love you, Livia darling, and that I'll love you as long as there's a breath of life in me. But save my life, I beg you, save it for yourself, if you love me.'

He took my hands and kissed them.

I was already persuaded. I went over to my writing-table to fetch the three little keys to my safe. I was afraid of making a noise, and walked on tiptoe even though I was barefooted. Remigio came with me into the study behind the alcove. I locked the door lest the count should hear, then opened the safe with some difficulty, for I was in such a state, and took out a complete set of diamonds, murmuring, 'Here, take them. They cost almost twelve thousand lire. Will you manage to sell them?'

Remigio took the jewellery case from my hand. He looked at the jewels and said, 'There are money-lenders everywhere.'

'It would be a shame to part with them for too little. Try and find some way of getting them back again.'

I was heartbroken. The tiara especially suited me so well.

'And will you give me the money as well?' asked Remigio. 'It would be useful.'

I searched in the safe for the gold napoleons, which I had stacked in a pile, and handed them to him, without counting them. He kissed me, and was about to rush off. I held him back. He pushed me away impatiently, saying, 'If you value my life, let me go.'

'Take care, can't you hear your boots squeak? In any case, wait. I need to see if the maid's there. She'll have to let you out.'

Sure enough, the maid was waiting in a nearby room.

'You'll write to me soon?'

'Yes.'

'Every other day?'

I wanted to give my lover, the man I loved so much, one last kiss; he was already gone.

I opened the windows and looked out into the street. The sun shone golden on the high mountainpeaks. The stable-boy and the scullery lad were standing in front of the gateway, talking. They looked up and saw me. Then they saw Remigio emerging from the house and hurrying away with his coat pockets bulging.

I went back to bed and cried all day long. I felt drained of energy. The next morning the doctor found that I had a temperature and was running a high fever. He prescribed quinine, which I did not take. I wanted to die. A whole week after Remigio's visit, the maid, as calm as ever, brought me a letter. As soon as I saw it, I snatched it from her hand. I had guessed it was from him – the first since his departure – and I sat down to read it with such frantic eagerness that when I came to the end I had to read it all over again; I had not taken any of it in.

I still remember it word for word, so often did the terrible events that followed give me cause to recall them:

'Beloved Livia,
You've saved my life. I sold the set of diamonds to some Shylock, for not much, to tell the truth, but in these times

of fear and turmoil it was impossible to get more than two thousand florins – enough to fill the doctors' voracious bellies. Before taking ill, I found a comfortable room near the Adige, in Via Santo Stefano 147, (write to me at this address). It is big and clean, with its own hallway leading directly onto the stairs. I have stocked up with tobacco, rum, playing cards and the entire works of Charles-Paul de Kock and Dumas. I've no lack of agreeable company, all male (don't panic), and all of them scroungers, and were it not for having to appear lame, and being unable to leave the house during the day, I would say that I was the happiest man in the world. Of course, there's one thing missing – your self, darling Livia, that I adore and would like to hold in my arms day and night. Well, now, don't worry about a thing. I shall read the news of the war, while having a smoke; and the more Italians and Austrians go to hell, the more I shall enjoy it. Love me always, as I love you. As soon as the war is over and these wretched doctors, who are costing me a tidy sum, leave me in peace, I shall come running to embrace you, more passionate than ever.

 Yours,
  Remigio'

The letter left me disconcerted and shocked, so vulgar did it seem. But then, poring over it, I gradually persuaded myself that the tone in which it was written was affectedly light and gay, and that my lover had made a painful but very noble effort to contain the violence of his own feelings, so as not to fan the flames of my already blazing passion, and in order to calm my mind a little, knowing how terribly anxious I was. I studied every phrase, every syllable of the letter. I had burned all the others almost as soon as I received them: this one I kept in a little pocket of my purse, and often took it out when I was alone, after locking myself in the room. Everything confirmed me in my wishful thinking: these expressions of love seemed all the more heartfelt for being hasty, and these coarse cynical remarks, I fancied, were sublime in their generous self-sacrifice. I so badly needed to believe in his infatuation, as an excuse for my own; and his cowardice thrilled my heart because I believed myself to be the cause of it. But my overheated imagination did not stop there. Who knows, I thought to myself, who knows whether this letter might not be all a well-intentioned deceit. Perhaps he has already gone to the battlefield, perhaps he is even now facing the enemy. But caring more for me than for himself, not wanting me to die of terror and dismay, he was allaying my fears by telling a white lie. The idea had no sooner occurred to me than I became obsessed with it. The insomnia, aversion to food, and physical ailments I was suffering contributed to a state of acute mental feverishness.

I was living in virtual solitude. My social circle had already been getting gradually more restricted, because for some time now the noble families of Trentino, opposed to the count's political opinions, had very politely but firmly been keeping their distance. The young people, being fervently nationalist, unceremoniously avoided us, indeed hated us. Local officials, not knowing how the war would end, and wary of compromising themselves one way or another, now avoided setting foot in our house. So, we were seeing a few pro-Austrian aristocrats, all of them penniless and parasitic, and a few high-ranking Tyrolese officials, who were crass, pig-headed and stank of beer and cheap tobacco. Army officers no longer had any free time to spare, nor any desire to spend it in my company.

My relationship with Remigio, which everybody but my husband knew about, had increased my isolation – an isolation that I actually welcomed, indeed needed, given the state of mind I had been living in for some while. Remigio had not written again since that memorable letter. I imagined him facing perils that seemed all the more horrible for being uncertain. I could perhaps have lived with the sure risks of battle, but the suspense of not knowing whether my lover was fighting or not was driving me mad. I wrote to Verona to a general I knew, to two colonels, then to one of those junior officers who had so long courted me in Venice: I received no reply. I sent Remigio countless letters: he never answered.

Meanwhile, hostilities began: civilian life was overridden; the railways and roads were solely for the use of munitions wagons, ambulance carts and supply trucks; of cavalry brigades that went by amid clouds of dust, artillery units that made the houses shake, and infantry regiments that kept coming, one after another, in an endless winding column, creeping along like a snake trying to encompass the whole world within its enormous coils.

One breathlessly hot morning, 26th June, came the first news of a dreadful battle: Austria was defeated, with ten thousand dead, twenty thousand wounded, the standards lost, and Verona, still ours, but, like the other strongholds, close to surrendering to the Italians' diabolical onslaught.

My husband was in the country and was to be away for a week.

I rang furiously; the maid did not come. I rang again; the butler appeared in the doorway.

'Are you all asleep? Lazy wretches! Send me the coachman, at once, do you hear?

A few minutes later an apprehensive-looking Giacomo arrived, buttoning up his livery.

'How many miles is it from here to Verona?'

He thought for a moment.

'Well?' I said, losing my temper.

Giacomo made his calculations. 'From here to Rovereto, about fourteen. From Rovereto to Verona must be . . . I don't know . . . with two good horses it would be ten hours, give or take a little, without counting the stops.'

'You've never driven with the horses from Trento to Verona?'

'No, signora contessa. I've done the journey from Rovereto to Verona.'

'It doesn't matter. I know myself that it's two hours to Rovereto from here.'

'Forgive me, signora contessa, two and a half.'

'So two and ten makes twelve in total.'

'Let's say thirteen, signora contessa, and going at a good pace.'

'How many horses has the count taken with him?'

'His usual black mare.'

'So there are four in the stables.'

'Yes, signora contessa: Fanny, Candida, Lampo and the stallion.'

'Could you harness all four of them?'

'Together?'

'Yes, together.'

Giacomo smiled with a benevolently pitying look. 'I'm sorry, signora contessa, that can't be done. The stallion . . .'

'Well, then, harness the other three.'

'Poor Lampo is lame, and can't even manage a brisk walk.'

'Then for God's sake, harness Fanny and Candida as usual,' I shouted, stamping my feet. Then I added, 'For tomorrow morning, at four.'

'As you wish, signora contessa. And, forgive me, so that I know how much fodder to take, where are we going?'

'To Verona.'

'Verona! God help us! In how many days?'

'By evening.'

'Forgive me, signora contessa, but that's just not possible.'

'And I insist on it, do you understand?'

I replied in such an imperious tone that the poor man scarcely had the courage to stammer out, 'Have a heart, signora contessa. It'll be the death of both horses, and the master will throw me out into the street.'

'I take full responsibility. Do as you're told and don't worry about anything else.' And I gave him four gold coins. 'I'll give you twice as much on our return, on condition that you don't breathe a word to anybody.'

'There's no danger of that. But what about the chaos on

the roads – the wagons and cannons, unruly soldiers, trouble from the police?'

'I'll worry about that.'

Giacomo bowed his head, resigned but not convinced.

'What time will we get to Verona?'

'That's in the hands of Providence, signora contessa. And it'll be a miracle if we all get there alive – you, signora contessa, me, and the two poor beasts. For me, it doesn't matter, but for you and the horses!'

'Well, at four o'clock then, and not a word. If you hold your tongue, you shall have what I promised. If you talk, I'll sack you on the spot, with no wages. Is that clear? See to it that everyone, including the chambermaid, thinks we're going to see Marchesa Giulia at San Michele.'

Wearing a gloomy expression, Giacomo bowed and left the room.

At dawn I was in the carriage, and on my way. I had drawn the curtains over the windows, and out of a corner I watched the gasping dusty foot-soldiers, who lined up along the ditches, thinking there was some important person in the coach; some of them gave a military salute.

From time to time, to my intense annoyance, we had to slow down, or actually stop for a few minutes to wait for heavy swaying wagons to get out of our way. However, things went much better than Giacomo had predicted. A mounted police patrol stopped the carriage, but when the sergeant saw there was a lady inside he contented himself with calling out chivalrously, 'Safe journey!' After Rovereto, at Pieve, we stopped to rest a little. Then, having unhitched the mares at Borghetto, for they could take no more, we spent a good three hours there that to me felt like three years, being cooped up inside the carriage as I was, listening to the complaining and swearing of the squads of soldiers who would collapse on the ground near the inn for a few moments, beneath the meagre shade of the stunted trees, to eat a crust of bread and take a swig of water. I must have called Giacomo ten times. He came to the window looking extremely disgruntled, forcing himself to appear calm. Then raising his hat, he kept saying, 'Another ten minutes, signora contessa.'

Eventually, we set off again, thank God. The River Adige, which we drove alongside, was almost dry; the fields looked parched; the road gleamed with a blinding whiteness; there was not a cloud to be seen in the blue skies. The sides of the carriage were burning hot and I felt suffocated in that oppressive heat and thick dust. My forehead was beaded with sweat, and I drummed my feet with impatience. I did not spare Chiusa a glance, but listened for the crack of Giacomo's whip. At Pescantina we stopped again for fresh horses: it was another ten long miles to Verona and the poor beasts could hardly walk. The sun had gone down in a fiery blaze. And still there were wagons and soldiers, police patrols, and the dust, with a deafening din and a screech of metal at times, and at other times a confused and fearful murmur, in which it was possible to distinguish groans and curses and verses of lewd songs sung by muffled voices. So far, we had been travelling with the tide of men and vehicles, now we passed a number of ambulance carts coming towards us, and several companies of walking wounded; soldiers with their arms in slings, and with bandages round their heads, pale-faced, stooped, limping, and in tatters. And Remigio? Remigio? I shouted to Giacomo to use the whip-handle on the horses. It was beginning to get dark.

We reached the walls of Verona at about nine. And so great was the panic, so great the confusion, that no one paid any attention to the carriage, and we were able to get to the Torre di Londra hotel without further hindrance. There was not a room to be had, not so much as a corner to sleep in, either in the hotel, or, so I was assured, in any other lodging house in the city: they had all been requisitioned for officers. The horses were tied up in the courtyard, more dead than alive; Giacomo was to attend to them. I jumped out of the carriage at last.

I had some young ragamuffin take me to number 147 in

Via Santo Stefano. We had to walk up and down the street several times, looking above the doorways, before we were able to discern the number of the house by the glimmer of the few streetlights.

If Remigio was at home, I wanted to surprise him. My limbs were all atremble with impatience and desire, but he might be in bed, he might be with someone, and although I desperately wanted to see him at once, yet I felt I ought to send the boy on ahead as a scout. He was crafty and understood immediately: he was to ring and ask for the lieutenant on a matter of the utmost urgency, insist that he open the door, go upstairs and tell him some story – for instance, that a gentleman whose name he had forgotten, who was staying at the Torre di Londra hotel, wanted news of his health, without delay. As the boy came out he was to leave open the door to Remigio's lodgings, as well as the street door. I hid by the side of the house, in an alleyway running from the road down to the river.

The boy rang the bell.

An angry voice came from the top floor.

'Who is it?'

'Is Lieutenant Ruz there?'

'It's the other bell, the middle one. Damn you!'

The boy rang the other bell. A minute went by that seemed to last for ever, and no one appeared. The boy rang again. Then from the second floor a woman's voice called out, 'Who is it?'

'Is Lieutenant Ruz there?'

'Yes, but he won't see anybody.'

'I need to speak to him.'

'Tomorrow morning, after nine.'

'No, this evening. Are you afraid of burglars?'

Another minute went by, and at last the door opened.

There was Remigio! My heart was bursting with joy. My eyes grew clouded and I had to lean against the wall for support. Shortly afterwards the boy returned. Remigio had sent him packing, but he had managed to leave both doors ajar. I regained control of myself, gave the cunning lad a few coins, and slipped into the house. I had thought to bring some matches with me: on the second floor landing there were two doors, with Remigio's visiting card pinned above one of them. I pushed it and it swung open, and without making a sound I entered a room that was practically dark. This was the culmination of all my hopes: I could already feel the arms of my lover – the man for whom I would unhesitatingly have given everything I owned, including my life – crushing me to his broad chest. I could feel his teeth biting into my skin, and I was overwhelmed in anticipation with ineffable bliss.

I felt weak with relief, and had to sit down on a chair in the hall. Hearing and seeing as if in a deep dream, I had lost all sense of reality. But someone nearby was laughing and laughing: it was a woman's laughter, shrill, coarse and boisterous, and it gradually roused me. I listened, rising from my seat, and, holding my breath, approached a door that stood wide open, through which I could see into a huge, brightly lit room. I was standing in shadow, out of sight. Oh, why did God not strike me blind at that moment? There was a table with the remains of a meal on it. Beyond the table was a big green sofa: there lay Remigio, playfully tickling a girl's armpit. She was hooting and shrieking with laughter, wriggling and writhing all over, trying in vain to free herself from his clutches, and he was kissing her on the arms, the neck, the nape – wherever he could.

I was incapable of moving: I was nailed to the spot, my eyes transfixed, my ears straining to hear, my throat dry.

The man, tiring of this game, grabbed the girl by the wrist and sat her on his lap. Then they began talking, often breaking off for caresses and playfulness. I heard the words, but their meaning escaped me. Suddenly the woman said my name.

'Show me the pictures of Contessa Livia.'

'You've seen them so many times already.'

'Show them to me, please.'

Without getting up from the sofa, the man lifted the

edge of the tablecloth, opened the drawer of the table, and took out some papers. The girl, who had now turned serious, searched through them for the photographs and gazed at them for a long time.

Then she said, 'Is Contessa Livia beautiful?'

'You can see she is.'

'You don't understand: I want to know whether you think she's more beautiful than I am.'

'To me, no woman could be more beautiful than you.'

'Look, in this photograph, her ballgown leaves her arms and shoulders completely bare, right down to here.' And the young girl rearranged her blouse, holding up the picture for comparison.

'Look, do you think I'm more beautiful?'

The man kissed her between her breasts. 'A thousand times more beautiful!' he exclaimed.

The girl stood by the lamp, staring at the man, who smiled at her, and she picked up the four pictures one by one and very slowly tore each of them into four pieces and let the shreds drop on to the table, amid the plates and glasses. The man kept smiling.

'But you also tell her that you love her, you devil.'

'You know I say it to her as little as possible. But I need her, and we would not be here together, darling, if she hadn't given me that money I told you about. Those wretched doctors made me pay dearly for my life.'

'How much were you left with?'

'Five hundred florins, some of which is already spent. I need to write to my treasure-house in Trento: one gold coin for every sweet word.'

'And yet,' said the woman, her eyes filled with tears, 'and yet it upsets me.'

The man drew her very close to him on the green sofa, murmuring, 'Now, I don't want any tears.'

At that point I had a complete change of heart: love turned to loathing. I found myself in the street, not knowing where I was going. I was jostled by groups of soldiers that passed me in the darkness. Stretchers went by, from which came long drawn-out groans or shrill cries of pain, and I saw a few scuttling townsfolk, a few frightened peasants. No one paid any attention to me, as I hugged close to the walls of the houses, dressed all in black with a thick veil over my face. I came to a broad avenue planted with shadowy trees, where the river, flowing on my right, cooled the breathless air a little. The water was almost lost in the shadows, but I was not tempted, even for one second, to commit suicide. Although I was not in the least aware of it, an ugly idea, as yet vague and indistinct, had already germinated within me, and it gradually invaded my heart and mind entirely: the idea of revenge.

I had given everything to that man. He had been my life. Without him, I had felt as though I would die; with him, I had been in heaven. And he gave his heart and kisses to another woman! The entire scene I had just witnessed was conjured up before me; I could still see that wanton lust before my very eyes. It was intolerable! For his sake I had come running, surmounting every obstacle, scorning every danger, casting my good name into the mud. I had come running to help him, to comfort him, and I find him safe and sound, more handsome than ever, in someone else's arms! And the pair of them – he who owes me everything, and his sweetheart – insult my dignity and love, and deride and ridicule me. And it is I who am paying for their orgies! That blonde minx brazenly boasts of being more beautiful than me, and (this was the supreme insult that really rankled) he himself proclaims her more beautiful!

All this emotion had left me weak: the anger boiling inside me had afflicted my whole body with a burning fever that made my legs tremble. I did not know where I was. I would not, could not, ask some passer-by to take me back to the inn, to be shut up inside the carriage again. I sat down on the riverbank, staring up at the dark sky. Unable to rest, I went back into the city-streets. I was going out of my mind. I was dropping with exhaustion, and had not eaten for eighteen hours. I happened to find myself outside a modest coffee-house. I passed in front of the window several times; it looked empty, so I went inside and sat down in the farthest and darkest corner, and ordered something.

In the opposite corner, lying stretched out on the narrow red banquette that ran all the way round that huge, damp, dimly lit, low-ceilinged room were two soldiers, smoking and yawning. Shortly afterwards another two officers came in: a tall, thin young man of maybe nineteen, with a neat moustache; and a stocky, thick-set fellow of about forty, who had a purple face, all lumps and warts, and coal-black, bushy eyebrows, while the moustaches under his big nose were so thick and coarse they looked like horsehair. He had in his mouth a short-stemmed Bohemian pipe with an enormous bowl that issued great clouds of smoke, rising one after the other, to darken the ceiling.

The young man went straight over to greet the officers in the corner. I heard him say, 'In the space of two hours I've seen forty men die on the operating table under the knife – the surgeons were tossing aside arms and legs as though playing ball, and they were trepanning and mending heads . . . '

'They should mend the heads of our generals,' growled the pipe-smoker sarcastically.

No one took any notice of me.

A girl came in, alone, who looked like a shop-girl, and she sat down beside the thin young officer. 'Will you buy me a coffee?' she asked him aloud.

After some conversation, to which I paid no attention, one of the two soldiers lying down said to the girl, without moving, 'You know, I saw that Lieutenant Remigio of yours, Costanza.'

'When?' asked the woman.

'Today. I went to visit him. He was with Giustina. Do you know her?'

'Yes, that fair-haired girl with three false teeth.'

'I've never noticed.'

'Take a good look at her. And how is Remigio?'

'He has the odd twinge in his leg that makes him yelp every now and then, and he limps a bit, that's all. A truly providential illness, that was. Other men are risking their lives, wearing themselves out with hunger and exhaustion in this infernal heat, suffering all the calamities of this war, while he has fun, eating and drinking, with someone to pay his keep.'

'Who on earth is keeping a wastrel like that?'

'A lady.'

'An old crone.'

'No, my dear, a beautiful young woman, a millionairess and a countess, what's more, who's madly in love with him.

'And she pays for the Lieutenant's amusements?'

'She gives him money – a lot of money.'

'Poor fool!'

'Remigio calls her his Messalina. He hasn't told me her family name, but he did say that she was from Trento and that her first name was Livia. Is there anyone here who knows Trento?'

The thin officer said, 'I'll ask round and let you know whatever I find out, tomorrow evening, assuming we're still in Verona by then. Contessa Silvia, was that it?'

'Livia, Contessa Livia, and don't forget,' shouted the recumbent officer.

Costanza spoke up again. 'But is Remigio really unwell then?'

'That's for sure. You see, no one can fool four doctors: one from Remigio's own regiment; one, selected by the general, from another regiment; and two from the military hospital. Every three days they go and visit him. They squeeze and tap and tug his leg, and make him yell. Once he fainted. He's better now.'

'He'll be cured as soon as the war's over,' Costanza insisted.

'Don't even say that as a joke,' said the other officer lying stretched out, who had not spoken till then. 'Let me tell you that if there were the least suspicion of chicanery the lieutenant and the doctors would be shot within twenty-four hours, one as a deserter from the field of battle, the others as accomplices and accessories.'

'And they would deserve it, by God!' roared the Bohemian without removing the pipe from his mouth.

The young officer added, 'General Hauptmann wouldn't even wait twenty-four hours.'

At these words the hazy idea already in my mind became vividly clear: I had found the solution.

'General Hauptmann,' I repeated to myself.

Overcome, as the blood rushed to my head, I was obliged to remove the veil completely from my face. I felt parched, and called for some water. Alerted to my presence, the officers immediately came crowding round me.

'Ah, what a beautiful woman!'

'Is there anything you need?'

'Would you like a glass of Marsala?'

'May we keep you company?'

'Are you waiting for someone?'

'What wonderful eyes!'

'Such lips were meant for kissing!'

The thin young officer had insinuated himself onto the banquette, next to me. Being the youngest, he wanted to prove himself the boldest. I freed myself from his clutches and tried to get up to leave, but two others held me back. The ugly Bohemian looked on, smoking his pipe. I turned to him and cried, 'Sir, I am a lady. Help me, and escort me back to the Torre di Londra.'

The Bohemian pushed his way over, and practically sent the young officer flying. Then, looking stern and serious, he put his pipe in his pocket and offered me his arm.

We left together. On the way to the hotel, which was not far, he said little, but spoke to me with respect. I asked him who General Hauptmann was, where he had his office, and further information that I had my own good reasons for wanting to know.

I learned that the General was commander-in-chief of

48

this stronghold, and that his Headquarters was based in Castel San Pietro.

The carriage entrance to the inn was still wide open although it was long past one in the morning. There was a great coming and going of soldiers and civilians. I thanked the officer, who reeked of infernal tobacco, and I made myself as comfortable as I could on the cushions in my carriage that stood in a corner of the yard. Being dead tired, I soon dozed off, but the sound of someone banging on the window woke me with a start.

The rough, coarse voice of the Bohemian was saying repeatedly, 'It's me, signora contessa. With all due respect, I'd just like a word with you.'

I lowered the window and the officer handed me something: it was my purse, which I had left behind on the table in the coffee-house in the confusion that had arisen when I was about to pay. His three companions had found it and given it to him.

He said solemnly, 'There's not a piece of paper or a single coin missing.'

'But were the papers read?' I was thinking of Remigio's letter, the only one I had kept and that, not for anything in the world, would I have wanted to let out of my hands.

'No, signora contessa. Your visiting-cards were seen, and the portrait of Lieutenant Remigio. Nothing else, on my honour.'

The following morning before nine I had Giacomo drive me in the carriage up to the Headquarters of the stronghold. It seemed an endless climb. I shouted to Giacomo to whip the horses. The square in front of the castle was crowded with all kinds of soldiers, casualties, and townspeople, but I reached the entrance to the offices unhindered. There, an old disabled soldier took my visiting-card. He returned a few minutes later, saying that General Hauptmann invited me to enter his private quarters, and that he would come and pay his respects as soon as he had dealt with some matters of the utmost urgency.

I was led through loggias, along corridors and across terraces to a room with three windows that looked out over the whole city. Broken into sections by its bridges, the Adige traced an S-shape, with one of its loops winding round the foot of the little hill on which Castel San Pietro stood, and the other round the foot of another dark, crenellated castle. And rising above the houses were the rooftops and towers of the ancient basilicas; and marked by a large open space was the vast oval of the Arena. The morning sun shone brightly on the town and hills, on one side turning the mountains golden, and on the other casting a serene light over the endless green plain scattered with white villages, houses, churches, and bell-towers.

Two little girls, with pink faces and straw-blonde hair, burst into the room, with great peals of laughter. When they saw me, they were shy at first, but then suddenly plucked up courage and came over to me.

The older one said, 'Please take a seat. Shall I fetch Mama?'

'No, my child, I'm waiting for your Papa.'

'We haven't seen Papa this morning. He's so busy.'

'I want to see Papa,' cried the little one. 'I love my Papa.'

At that point the General came in, and the little girls went running up to him, and clung to his legs, and tried to climb on to his shoulders. He picked up each child in turn and kissed her; and his two madcap daughters laughed, while two tears of blissful tenderness welled up in the General's eyes. He turned to me, saying, 'Forgive me, signora. If you have children, you'll understand.'

He sat down opposite me and added, 'I know the count by name, and should be delighted to be of any service to the signora contessa.'

I made it clear to the General that the children should leave us, and in a voice full of gentleness he said to them, 'Run along now, girls, run along, the contessa and I have things to discuss.'

The children took a step towards me as if they were

about to kiss me. I turned away. They finally went off, looking a little upset.

'General,' I murmured, 'I've come to do my duty as a loyal citizen.'

'Is the signora contessa German?'

'No, I'm from the Trentino.'

'Ah, very well, then!' he exclaimed, gazing at me with a somewhat astonished and impatient air.

'Read this.' And with a decisive gesture I handed him Remigio's letter, which I had found again in the pocket of my purse.

Having read the letter, the General said, 'I don't understand. Is the letter addressed to you?'

'Yes, General.'

'So the man who wrote it is your lover.'

I did not reply. The General drew a cigar from his pocket and lit it. He leapt up and began to pace round the room. All of a sudden he planted himself in front of me, and staring into my face, he said, 'Well, be quick, I'm in a hurry.'

'The letter is from Remigio Ruz, Lieutenant of the 3rd Grenadiers.'

'And?'

'The letter is clear. He passed himself off as sick, by paying the four doctors.' And in a voice quickened with hatred, I added, 'He is a deserter from the field of battle.'

'I see. The Lieutenant was your lover and he has jilted you. You're taking your revenge by having him shot, and the doctors along with him. Is that it?'

'I don't care about the doctors.'

The General stood there for a while, thinking, with a frown on his face, then he handed back the letter I had given him.

'Signora, consider this carefully: it's dishonourable to act as an informer, and what you are doing is murder.'

'General,' I exclaimed, looking up at him haughtily, 'carry out your duty.'

★

At about nine o'clock that evening a soldier delivered a note to me at the Torre di Londra hotel, where a room had finally been found for me. It read as follows:

'Tomorrow morning, at four thirty precisely, Lieutenant Ruz and his regiment's doctor will be shot in the second courtyard of Castel San Pietro. This letter will grant you access to witness the execution. The undersigned regrets that he cannot also offer the signora contessa the spectacle of the other two doctors' execution. For reasons that it would be futile to explain here, they have been referred to another court martial.

General Hauptmann'

At three thirty I left the hotel on foot, in the pitch dark, accompanied by Giacomo. I told him to leave me at the bottom of the hill of Castel San Pietro, and I began to climb the steep road alone. I was hot, I could not breathe. I did not want to remove the veil from my face. Instead I undid the top buttons of my dress and tucked the flaps inside. With the air on my breast I was able to breathe more easily.

The stars were growing pale, as dawn came, diffusing its yellow light. I followed some soldiers round the side of the castle and into a courtyard enclosed within high, forbidding outer walls. Two squads of grenadiers were already lined up, motionless. No one took any notice of me, in the semi-darkness, amid the silent throng of soldiers.

I could hear the bells ringing down in the city, and a confusion of sound rising from below. A low door in the castle creaked open and two men came out, with their hands tied behind their backs. One of them, a thin, dark-haired fellow, stepped forward boldly, with his head held high. The other, flanked by two soldiers supporting him with great difficulty by the armpits, dragged his feet, sobbing.

What happened next, I do not know. Something was read out, I think. Then there was a deafening noise and I saw the dark young man fall to the ground, and in the same instant I noticed that Remigio was stripped to the waist, and I was blinded by those arms, shoulders, neck, and limbs that I had so loved. Into my mind flashed a picture of my lover, full of ardour and joy, when he held me for the first time in his steely embrace, in Venice at the Sirena. I was startled by a second burst of sound. On his chest that still quivered, whiter than marble, a blonde woman had thrown herself, and was spattered with spurting blood.

At the sight of that shameless hussy all my anger and resentment returned to me, and with them came dignity and strength. I had acted within my rights, and I turned to leave, serene in the self-respect that came from having fulfilled a difficult duty.

As I was going through the gate I felt the veil being torn from my face. I turned and saw before me the unsightly features of the Bohemian officer. He removed the stem of his pipe from his huge mouth, and with his moustaches coming at me, he spat on my cheek . . .

Did I not say that young lawyer Gino would be back? All it took was one line – 'Come, let's be friends again' – to bring him running. He jilted that child-bride of his a week to the day before the marriage was to take place. And embracing me almost with Lieutenant Remigio's strength, he keeps telling me over and over again, 'Livia, you're an angel!'

A BODY

I

Whether my beloved were nymph or sprite, I do not know. In the words of an old popular verse, I called her 'the capricious young lady of the flowery fields'. She was eighteen. Every so often she would let go of my arm and run off across those lovely green grass lawns in the Prater. Sometimes I chased after her, and she would dodge away, circling round the enormous trunk of an oak-tree, or bounding off in all directions like a gazelle. Sometimes I let her go, and then, seeing how far away from me she was, she would stop, lie down on the grass, and wait for me, out of breath.

As I came up to her, I looked all around to see if anyone might be watching. Propping herself up on her arms, she arched her supple body, which curved like the handle of a Greek vase. I bent down and kissed her.

Then I said to her, 'Watch out, Carlotta, your garters are showing.'

And springing to her feet, she shook the skirt of her pink dress, and whispered in my ear with sweet irony, 'Are you jealous of the rising moon?'

We were actually quite alone in that corner of the park, and the rays of the moon were beginning to outshine the sunset's reddish glow. A sound of great merriment, of music and singing, could be heard in the distance: the numerous voices of a jubilant crowd. Through the leafy branches we saw a lamp come on, then another, and yet another, and so it continued, until the shape of the trees stood out black against a bright blaze of yellow light. 'Let's stop here,' said Carlotta. 'We can sit on this bench. Don't you feel an utterly serene sense of enchantment in your heart and somehow a great desire for solitude?' And she sighed softly, and squeezed my hand, and looked up at the sky with liquid, smiling eyes. I was about to reply, but the sound of someone coming by silenced me. A tall, thin man dressed in black passed in front of us. Carlotta stifled a cry at the sight of him and clung to my body, all atremble.

'What is it, my darling?' I asked very anxiously.

'Nothing, nothing,' replied Carlotta. 'I was afraid. It was childishness. Forgive me.'

And clasping her round the waist, I tried to make her sit down again, but she broke away, saying, 'Please, let's go to the Wurstel-Prater. I need to have some fun.' She grabbed hold of my hand and, practically running, dragged me into the midst of the crowd and into the light.

In response to my questions she said that it was just a silly scare, and she promised to explain some other time.

'But has that man done you any harm?' I insisted.

'No.'

'Has he tried to make advances?'

'Oh no, no!'

'But tell me at least whether he has ever spoken to you?'

'Never, I swear to you.'

'Well?'

'It's foolishness, I tell you. I'll explain tomorrow. Right now, I'm sorry, but I don't want to think about it.' And she planted herself right in front of a puppet booth.

It was one of the usual farces, with a girl who hides her lovers in the flour-bin, a devil that steals wine and dishes from the table, while an old woman who keeps replacing the plates and bottles gets beaten by the devil, and other such childish things. Then a coffin appeared on the stage and two undertakers chased the old woman into it, and nailed her in with a hammer. And afterwards they put the coffin on their shoulders and were about to leave, when all of a sudden the lid flew open and a rabbit, a real white rabbit, jumped out, to gales of laughter from the children, their nursemaids, and the corporals and sergeants glad-eyeing the young women. Carlotta, who had calmed down a little and begun to smile, was upset again by the ending and asked me to take her away.

In the four months that we had been together, I had noticed that despite her cheerful disposition and good health Carlotta had a great fear of death. Everything that could possibly remind her of it, one way or another, was enough to make her pale and tremble. She never wanted to go anywhere near a hospital, and once, when we were on our way to the Augarten in a carriage, I told the coachman to turn into a side-street so as not to pass too close to the Hospital of the Brothers of St John, on Taborstrasse. If she saw a funeral procession in the distance, she would turn back or take refuge in a shop, and look the other way. She did not want to read about the dead or the sick, or hear any talk of them. She tolerated the company of doctors, but could not stand to be with surgeons. And in a beer-house one day, when Dumreicher was telling me, in the course of conversation, about some unusual autopsy case, Carlotta, who was with me, suddenly felt unwell. She quickly recovered, but for twenty-four hours those pretty lips of hers refused to form their usual smile. I took such instances of odd behaviour to be a spontaneous expression of extreme sensitivity. I forgave them, I respected them. As a matter of fact I found them pleasing in that artless soul.

Yet, though she had the soul of a child, she had the body of a goddess. Comparison with Greek statues can no more than suggest those slender, vigorous limbs of tempered steel. She was like the Amazons and the Huntress Dianas of Scopas and Praxiteles; she also had the poise of callipygean Venuses, of crouching Venuses, of reclining nymphs, of Psyche embracing Cupid. Cleomenes, son of Apollodoros, surely taught her how to pose, after he had put the finishing touches to the Medici Venus.

Her face was reminiscent of the head of that lovely Euterpe in the Berlin Museum: her nose ran in a straight line from her brow, with only the slightest curve; her elongated eyes, set a little higher towards the middle of her face, looked as though drawn with the arc of a compass; her closed lips were slightly down-turned at the corners of her mouth, with two barely perceptible lines running to her nostrils; while her chin and cheeks described the inverted curve of a perfect parabola. The statue of Euterpe has curly hair, presumably blonde. Carlotta's hair was blonde and curly, and she wore it tied back, like that of the antique statue, with two heavy braids circling her brow and covering her ears. However, there was in Carlotta's face none of that rather disdainful and solemn coldness almost always the characteristic of Greek faces. In her case, the Attic perfection of form bore the mark of a true, easy and candid gaiety. And light-blue eyes completed the portrait of this ingenuous creature.

As for her colouring, Titian's splendour and Van Dyck's subtlety could not have captured it. Wonderful transitions, almost from blue to vermilion, registered upon that snowy-whiteness: beneath that smooth, fresh, transparent skin there was passionate life flowing. This woman was the embodiment of grace, vigour, and health. When I was out with Carlotta in Vienna, that city of beautiful women, people would turn in admiration. One morning, on the Graben, that strange fellow Raal, who was then painting the frescoes in the Arsenale, suddenly burst out with these words: 'Ah, if only she could have been the model for my Germania!' And he bowed to her, respectfully raising his hat.

The Wurstel-Prater was full of opera-houses, play-houses, circuses, cabarets, cycloramas, magic lanterns, coffee-shops, concert halls, shooting booths, menageries, photographers' galleries, street musicians, strolling players, acrobats, pedlars selling all kinds of things; and most of all of beer-houses. Thousands upon thousands of people wandered about, stopping here and there, some entering one booth, some another, buying this or that; jostling and crowding, and treading on each other's feet, always with tolerant good-humour, with rough but fulsome courtesy. Laughter came as easily to those fleshy lips as beer went down those throats. The beer-houses were packed – some consisting of sumptuous rooms festooned and garlanded and adorned with silk and velvet, whilst others comprised a small wooden hut and a vast area marked out by a fence, with tables and chairs scattered all about. Anyone who could not find a seat settled down on the trampled grass. The slim, young serving-girls rushed to and fro non-stop, carrying glass mugs – ten at a time – brimful of silver-foaming, amber beer. A variety of lamps, torches, chandeliers, paper-lanterns of a hundred different colours and shapes illuminated that vast scene: in one area everything was bathed in light; a little way off everything was shrouded in virtual darkness. Looking up, you could see the dewy leaves on the big trees glistening and the heavenly heights twinkling. There was something mysterious about that Babel-like din, that infernal racket. Suddenly, amidst the welter of speech and guffaws of laughter from so many countless mouths, the harmonious strains of an orchestra reached the ear, or the raucous sound of the tightrope-walkers' trumpet, or the sibilant note of a mouse-trainer's pipe, or the roar of a lion in its cage, or the howling of a stray dog.

The Wurstel-Prater was Carlotta's supreme delight. She enjoyed everything. She laughed heartily at the antics of the clowns, stood open-mouthed in front of the puppets, and insisted on listening to the mountebanks' patter from beginning to end. Once she made me climb into the narrow seat of a swing with her; then into a carriage on one of the carousels, and as we whirled round at top speed to the sound of a huge organ – I was almost beginning to feel dizzy – she playfully pointed out to me the two wooden dolphins that were supposed to be pulling us, and with childish glee she compared herself to Anphitrion and me to Neptune. The only thing she did not like were the wax-works.

But that evening Carlotta was in a different mood. She seemed troubled by some vexing thought; her gaze was distracted, and she hardly smiled. Close to a circus, where I wanted to take her, knowing how much she liked horses, we heard several voices greeting us. It was the whole family – father, mother, five children, housemaid and cook

– of the solemn clerk at the Census Office who rented us a part of his house: four rooms on Franz-Josefs-Quai, by the broad Danube Canal. They were on their way to catch the bus home, and Carlotta asked me to let her go back with them, saying that she felt a bit tired; that in an hour's time I would find her more cheerful than ever, and (this she murmured with a divine smile) she would be even more loving than usual.

I was left on my own in the midst of the throng.

II

I slowly made my way to a modest beer-house, away from the noise, where one of my dearest and closest friends, Dr Herzfeld, was in the habit of imbibing eight or nine mugs of beer at exactly this time of day. He was ten years older – or, to put it more kindly, less young – than me, and I was then aged twenty-four. He was short, fat, red-faced, with a pair of sparkling blue eyes.

He practised medicine, and I was a painter. Between our respective fields of study, there was one area of common ground: anatomy – for which he had no inclination, and to which I felt an almost insuperable aversion. This repugnance had driven my old art-master to distraction, and made me the butt of my fellow students' jokes. So, now and again, to prove my will-power and nerve, I had forced myself to tackle osteology, myology and other disciplines relating to the human body. Carlotta, to whom I never mentioned such unpleasant and depressing matters, had for the past four months been partly responsible for keeping me away completely from this gruesome research.

Herzfeld was not alone. He was talking to another man. As soon as he caught sight of me, he leapt up and came rushing towards me. 'It's ages since we last saw each other,' he said.

'I've been very busy,' I replied, 'although I've been wanting to see you for some time.'

'Yes, yes,' replied Herzfeld with one of his grimaces, which was intended to look sardonic, but was full of good-naturedness. 'Yes, you're busy being the happiest man on earth. I forgive you. Please God that you never have need of friends again, or of beer.' And he gave me his glass, with the froth still foaming on it, which a rosy-cheeked young girl had just brought him. Then, presenting me to the gentleman who was with him, he told him my name, and introducing the gentleman to me, in a voice full of respect he uttered the single syllable, 'Gulz.'

'Karl Gulz?'

Rising to his feet, the man gave a small, affirmative nod.

'Karl Gulz, the anatomist?'

He gave another nod, and sat down again, having waved at me to do likewise.

There were two reasons for my amazement. Karl Gulz was already a famous name among German scientists and artists. His magnificent work on aesthetic anatomy had been published more than three years ago, and during one of my brief periods of arduous anatomical study I had read it from cover to cover. Now, whereas I expected him to be a man well advanced in age, the person I saw before me was a youth of almost childlike appearance. He was tall of stature, but extremely thin, like a boy grown too fast for his age. He wore glasses, and on closer inspection there were a few lines visible on his forehead, but he had extremely fair, wavy hair that came down over the collar of his black coat, and his chin was graced with nothing but a little yellow fuzz that looked like his first growth of beard. A sad, absorbed calmness was registered upon his countenance. Then I noticed that, when he spoke, his nose, which had a slight aquiline curve to it, gave his face a rather peculiar expression of rigid and almost sinister determination, an expression reinforced by the character of his voice, which had a soft sound, but came in bursts, with an impassioned edge to it.

The second reason for my amazement lay in the vague similarity between Karl Gulz and the man whose features I had not been able to distinguish an hour ago in the shadows of twilight, and who had caused Carlotta to tremble and cry out. Had Carlotta known that he was an anatomist? Could that be why, being so squeamish, she had been overcome with such fear? But was I not, perhaps, more likely deceived by a superficial likeness of stature, thinness, bearing, and dress?

This amazement and these suspicions passed straight through my mind in a flash, and it cost me no effort to offer Gulz warm praise for his book, which, I said, had advanced both art and science.

He replied with great simplicity, but with deep conviction. 'That book, sir, is a youthful work, weak and inconclusive. My new theory required a great deal of evidence and very extensive development. I am now working on it, and with Nature's assistance the work will be finished in seven years' time.'

'And meanwhile you live amongst corpses?'

'A regular ten hours a day. In the nine years since I've been researching the beauty of the human body, I don't remember having stolen even a few hours from my precious studies, except on a handful of occasions, and then through no fault of mine, I assure you. Time taken up during the day in search of live models, and in studying them, can be made up at night. But unfortunately, Fate isn't often willing to favour me. Unfortunately, it very rarely happens that perfect models end up on my white marble slab!'

'For nine years you've been studying the human body, Doctor! You must have been very young when you began your anatomical investigations.'

'When I first began to work on the human body I was a little over twenty, but I had worked on other animals since I was a boy. I lived in the country and my father was a vet. I remember that as soon as lunch was over I would rush off to do my homework in a kind of stable all of my own that was full of birds, hens, and rabbits. Once I had finished yawning over my grammar and arithmetic, I would become engrossed in my childhood investigations and experiments. At about ten in the evening, my father used to come and fetch me by the ears, and drag me off to bed. Often I would wait until everyone was asleep, then get up again, and quietly tiptoe back to my stable, where sometimes the cry of one of my animals would betray me, and I would tearfully have to forgo the results of my experiment. Later, I moved on to dogs, cats, horses . . .'

Herzfeld, who had been listening in silence until then, broke in, saying, 'And you published an article in the *Universal Review of Anatomy*, entitled 'An anatomical investigation into the moral disposition of domestic animals'.'

'Quite so. I was sixteen when I wrote it.'

'I know the article. It's the work of an old man, not the work of a child. But anyone who wanted to deduce the individual character of a man from his bones and muscles . . .'

'. . . would to some extent be doing what I myself am doing,' said Gulz. 'And I'm not the first, for there have been hundreds of others, before and since Gall and Lavater, who have undertaken the same research.'

'But with what results, Doctor?'

'Very limited, it's true. Because their methods were inadequate. It's not just the external form of the body or the shape of the skull that need to be examined, but the entire human machinery. Everything is connected, it's all one and the same. That which most people call the mind is indistinguishable from what everyone is accustomed to call matter.'

'Thought is matter! How do you prove that, Doctor?' I asked, taking up the conversation.

'And, if you'll forgive me, how do *you* prove that thought is spirit? What is this spirit that you speak of, what is this mind? Man's vanity has tried to create for itself some indefinable attribute, distinct from molecules and the forces of nature. The idea of such an attribute is abhorrent, because it breaks the laws of the universe, and it's bound to seem puerile, because ultimately it's meaningless and explains nothing. Doesn't it seem to you more natural to believe that thoughts and feelings are nothing but the infinite and extremely rapid combinations, in every little brain-cell, of infinitely small atoms, which move, group together, break apart, reassemble, become dormant, and reawaken? It thus becomes easy to explain sleep, dreams, memory, sudden recollections, flights of fancy, the disciplined exercise of judgement, and so on.'

'And death?'

'Death is the putrefaction of thought-matter: the putrefaction of the mind.'

'What about passion? What about Man's genius?'

'From just ninety numbers, more than forty-three million five-number sequences can be formed. Given there are billions and billions of thought-molecules, surely their various combinations can account for all human genius, knowledge and passions.'

'What about the mother who weeps for her sick child, or the woman embracing her lover, and Goethe writing *Faust*, and Dante Alighieri dictating *The Divine Comedy* . . .'

'Special complex crystallizations, so to speak; phenomena whose whys and wherefores have not yet been discovered. They will be.'

'And, forgive me, Doctor, will we then be able to recreate, in a physics or chemistry or anatomy laboratory, the mental processes of a Goethe and a Dante, a mother's tears, or a young bride's smile?'

'In small part – who knows? But admittedly, in very small part . . .'

'I should think so, too.'

'. . . because Man has infinitely lesser means at his disposal than lie within the power of Nature, and because Nature's skill is infinitely superior to that which we command. For instance, we know of what substance the rose is made, how it germinates, nourishes itself, breathes, grows, flowers, and propagates. Yet, even though a rose does not think, are we able to recreate a rose for ourselves? Mind you, instruments are now becoming more sophisticated and Man's eye more expert. Already, with a simple electric current, we know how to reproduce the expressions of life on the face of a corpse: a smile, a sneer, a look of contempt, of wounded pride, a severe frown, the grimace of someone catching a bad smell, or the serene radiance of a joyful face. The voltaic battery, the microscope, chemical reagents, surgical operations, medical observations – what marvellous advances have not contributed to the study of the human body? And has not greater advantage yet to be taken of magneticism and – who knows? – of some other fluid as yet overlooked? Who can say to science: this is the limit? Who would ever have guessed that with the aid of a small glass prism a man would be capable of discovering, as he did a few years ago, that some elements, previously unknown to him and to any other human being on earth, could be made to burn in the sunlight? The sun has enabled us to find rubidium, caesium, thallium, and indium. We conduct experiments with the sun – what more is there to be said! There's just one master we ought to bow down and worship: and that is Science . . . '

As he spoke, Karl Gulz's face had assumed a solemn and mystical expression. His eyes shone and his brow seemed enormous. At the word 'Science', he had risen to his feet and, removing his hat, looked up to heaven. 'There's a priest in that man,' I thought, and I bowed my head in respect.

After a brief pause he went on. 'I live for science. I've never loved, suffered, rejoiced for anything but science. In my hour of joy, I embrace it; in my hour of distress, I invoke it; in my hour of pride, I raise an altar to it. But the man who studies feels that his hands are tied. It's true, we're no longer in the days of Vesalius, who had to disinter half-putrefied cadavers by night, in the Cemetery of the Innocents, or remove from the gallows of Montfaucon bodies already devoured more or less by crows and vultures. And but for such sublime audacity on his part, mankind would not have that famous treatise by Notomia, published in Basle, in 1543 . . . '

'With drawings by Calcar, I believe?'

'Precisely. And Vesalius was sentenced by the Tribunal of the Inquisition to make a penitential pilgrimage to Jerusalem, just because he thought it necessary, in order to verify his hypothesis, to break open the ribcage of a man whose heart was still beating.'

'It's a horrifying thing to have done.'

'Horrifying, why? I don't suppose you're horrified or that you cry shame and sacrilege when, through the wilfulness of a minister or prince, in order to conquer a piece of land that one nation steals from another, thousands upon thousands of men – who only a short while before were fine, honest, healthy young men – die in the most terrible anguish, out in the field with the sun beating down upon them, or in some pestilential hospital room. What is the benefit to humanity? What good will it do their grandchildren? So many wasted opportunities for experiments! You complain that doctors are ignorant, and you don't allow them to study.

'Who was the more human: the great Napoleon when he gave the orders for those glorious and pointless bloodbaths, or Ptolemy when he gave the physician Herophilus more than six hundred criminals, already condemned to death, to be dissected alive, so that science should derive some benefit from their bodies – a science that over the centuries has served the lives of millions of men. Cosimo de' Medici, a refined Florentine, did the same for the physician Fallopius. And was Fallopius, who carried out live experiments solely for love of science, any more barbarous than you, Herzfeld, or me, who for a discourteous word would run a man through, without scruple?

'You know,' Gulz rushed on with feverish enthusiasm, still addressing me, 'you know that in order to depict Prometheus being torn to pieces by the vulture, Parrhasius bought an old and venerable prisoner, then had him brought to his studio and proceeded to slash his liver with a sharp blade, and while the old man died in atrocious agony, the unruffled artist observed, studied and painted.'

'I know. It's a spine-chilling story that defies belief.'

'It's told by Seneca, who admittedly was not afraid of death, and he tells it as though it were something quite ordinary and completely natural. The fact is, those men of ancient times ranked the passion for truth above every other. For them, science had tremendous rights. Humanity counted for more than any man. In their understanding of the good they showed great courage and iron will, with no womanish sentimentality, or childish fears, or weak-minded scruples. They were men.'

With these words the young man rose to his feet, threw back his long hair with a toss of his head, offered his hand to Herzfeld, bowed to me, and turning his back on us, walked off without another word.

I was left stunned, half amazed and half sickened. But Herzfeld, seizing me by the arm and shaking me hard, said, 'Wake up, and let's go. Don't you see that we're alone now?' We hurried off.

Carlotta was waiting for me, but she was not very talkative that evening and in no mood for laughter, and she went to bed early.

III

Three days later Carlotta was her old self, more cheerful than ever. Only very occasionally, with a smile of compassion, did I think about Karl Gulz, of whom I had said nothing to my sensitive darling.

I put the finishing touches to a large painting, which was already in its huge frame. Every now and again I stepped back from the canvas to look at it with gratification. I took a mirror and, turning round, stood for a while happily contemplating in it the reflection of the painting. Then rushing over to Carlotta, to kneel before her and kiss her hand, I said to her, 'You've revealed to me my artistic talent: either this painting is all your work, or you yourself are a creation of my mind.' And for the thousandth time I scrutinized her, from her forehead to her pink toenails, with a long, searching look, though my eyes were full of sincere respect and the purest admiration.

The sunlight shining directly through the large window, catching the painting in its brightness, made the gold of the frame glisten, and illuminated Carlotta's divine body with a light full of reflections that, without the vulgar contrasts of an exaggerated chiaroscuro, allowed a fine appreciation of those graceful curves and that most delicate colouring. The modelling of the limbs had been done with a graver. Where the bones were not enveloped in solid muscle and flesh, and their ivory tint showed through beneath the skin (at the patella for instance, and between the ulna and humerus, and at the ileum and clavicle, and on the frontal bone); and in the delicate tracery of those slightly bluish veins on that pink complexion, (which had cost me immense pains of the sweetest kind) my palette had reached such perfection that I was enraptured. Carlotta bewitched me even more in my painting that in reality. I was so carried away with conceit that for a few moments that the woman herself seemed to me to be the living copy of my own handiwork. Half jokingly and half mystically, with my arms raised to heaven like those entreating figures in the catacombs, I declaimed in a loud voice a verse containing what I believe to be the definition of such a splendid creature – a verse by Terence, from *The Eunuch*:

'*Color verus, corpus solidum et suci plenum.*'

But meanwhile Carlotta had risen and very quietly come up behind me, throwing her arms round my shoulders and placing her hands over my mouth. I turned round at once, but she had already run to her room, locking the door behind her. A quarter of an hour later, she reappeared, wearing her pink dress.

The Arethusa in my painting was an exact likeness of Carlotta. I had completed this life-size portrait and the background landscape in just two months, working four hours a day, since I wanted to paint only with the sun in the room. And during those two months the sun been good enough to oblige me every day. The canvas was broader than it was tall. A patch of blue sky was visible between the leaves and branches of a tamarind grove, but the foreground was cast in diffused and almost luminous shadow, and there, like a gentle brook amidst the green clover, tender myrtle and red roses – 'What beautiful thing exists without the rose?' – lay the body of the nymph. To save her from the amorous pursuit of Alpheus, Diana turned her into a fountain, but Love, more ingenious than the goddess, at once taught her pursuer to turn himself into a river. And the waters of the fountain and river mingled together, and thus conjoined beneath the salt sea waves, welled up again, as the clearest of fresh water, upon the shores of Sicily. This elegant myth appealed to me in those days, and echoing blessed Anacreon, I kept repeating these of his verses:

'I would like to be a necklace round your lovely neck,
Or a girdle close round your bosom;
Or turn into a simple shoe,
If your foot would only tread upon me.'

Alpheus had done even better. And I wanted to depict the two lovers who became one. But when I set to work, I had first of all excluded Diana, and then left out Alpheus. And gradually the legend was reduced to a single name. Upon that name, moreover, I brought all my love and creative talent to bear. I conjured Arethusa as Faust had conjured Helen.

The nymph reclined in her grassy riverbed, her limbs following the earth's contours. With her left arm stretched out on the ground, supporting her head, her hair flowed down like waves of gold, and her right hand was tucked beneath her chin, while her bosom softly pressed down upon the brightly coloured flowers. And from her raised shoulder, the line of her body dipped deeply, in an ineffable curve, then rose again along her rounded haunch and continued in short planes and delicate sweeps, down to her feet.

On her face was an expression of newfound love, a mixture of serenity and sadness: a smile and a sigh.

'Bravo, my artist,' said Carlotta. 'I'm very proud to look so beautiful. But you must paint me again, a hundred different ways – dressed as an odalisk, a nun, a vestal virgin, Eve – in the countryside, in the dense groves of the Brühl Valley, where you won't have me posing on a boring divan covered with faded green cloth, but in the tall, emerald-green grass.'

'Yes, and what if someone came by?'

'Let them. Don't you want to put this Arethusa of ours on show in the Exhibition?'

'Yes, of course. It's to be the foundation-stone of my renown. But who knows? Men, and especially artists, are so prone to deluding themselves . . . '

'You monster! After all, you said that I'd done this painting for you. I don't want my skills called into question, you know. Now, if you want to display Arethusa for all to see, and say that Arethusa is actually me . . . '

'That's a different matter,' I replied curtly.

But Carlotta, who saw me frown, said with a ringing laugh, 'Can't you take a joke?' Then without a pause, she went on, 'When are we going to the country?'

'The painting's finished. Once I've put a coat of varnish on the roses, I'm going to write my name in the corner, here, over this stone.'

'Oh, no, you're not. I want to write your name myself.'

'You can, if you like. Then I shall send the painting to the Exhibition early tomorrow morning, and set off for Mödling before midday.'

'On your own?'

'On my own, if you don't mind. I shall quickly look for a little country house round there. It'll take me three days at most. Meanwhile, you can pack the trunks, see to my paints, canvases and paint-brushes. I'll come and fetch you, and we'll leave straightaway. Are you happy with that?'

'Yes. But do please find me a country house in the Brühl Valley, one with a lovely green pergola beside it. Oh God, if only you could find a jasmine pergola! And you will write to me from Mödling tomorrow evening, won't you?'

'I'll write to you, my lovely goddess. But you write, too, and post the letter early, the day after tomorrow, so that when I get back to the inn that evening I'll hear your voice saying good-night to me.'

And as we went on talking in this vein, I continued to add some final touches to the painting, while she first came and stood behind me, then went and stretched out on the divan, now getting up to look at her flowers on the balcony, and now skimming through some books and newspapers. And so the evening passed, and the next morning I sent the painting to the Exhibition, as planned, and left for Mödling.

The thought of spending the summer and autumn months with Carlotta in an isolated country villa, in the midst of a lovely wooded and mountainous landscape, filled me with joy. What fine plans I made for idleness and activity! How I reconciled in my imagination blissful indolence and zealous work! Sometimes I envisaged a Theocritan idyll: white goats beneath an oak, and bagpipes, and a painted jug filled with wine, and honey and honeycombs. And then I conceived of a hundred subjects for new paintings: the Nibelungen, the Bible, mythology, allegory, history. I did not stop to dwell on anything. My imagination raced on, like a wagon in which I was a passenger, its fancies speeding past like telegraph poles. Yet there was a common thread running through all these vagrant thoughts: the desire for beauty.

While lunching at Mödling, I enquired about houses for rent in the vicinity. There were several still available in the direction of Laxenburg and Baden, but I focused my attention on a villa consisting, I was told, of eight elegantly furnished rooms, with a garden and pergolas, and situated outside the quiet village of Teufelsmühle, in the very Brühl Valley so close to Carlotta's heart. I ordered a carriage for the following morning, and wrote two jubilant pages to my Arethusa.

When I came out of the inn to go for a walk before bedtime, I saw the snow on the peak of Mount Schneeberg glistening in the setting sun. Walking very slowly, humming to myself, allowing free rein to my imagination, and staring up at the sky – a sky extending through a range of infinitely subtle shades to the mysterious blue of night – I entered the narrow mountain-gorge called, as so often, Klausen. The pinkish limestone rocks, half bare, half covered with shadowy plants, loomed increasingly large in the darkness, until they seemed enormous, closing in and bearing down upon me more and more. As the shadows deepened, my thoughts, previously so cheerful, grew dejected and gloomy, until, goodness knows why, the lugubrious spectre of Karl Gulz invaded my mind. I hurried back to the inn, gulped down three or four glasses of beer, and being tired, fell asleep straightaway.

The next day, like the nightingale, I woke up singing. I had never felt my heart brimming with more resolute hope. My body and mind were fresh and nimble, bright and lively. The atmosphere around me was one of smiling happiness. While I was waiting for the carriage, first strolling along the road, then stretching out on the grass, the three leaves of a three-leafed clover seemed to me sublime; and a pebble, picked out in the shadow of the inn by a ray of sunshine, I thought a miracle. I had never been so alive to colour as I was then. In the greenness of a leaf, in the smooth, ultramarine blue of the sky, in the stains on the walls, I detected a refined art that had the same effect on me as Beethoven's music. The thousand graduations of colour each in itself revealed something new, suggested an idea, or roused a feeling within me. My sharpened vision had discovered a series of secret correlations with my spirit. Sorrow makes the poet, but joy makes the artist.

The villa near Teufelsmühle was truly charming. The Greek-style facade had a pronaos of four columns supporting a pediment, with a garlanded harp in bas-relief in the middle of the typanum. Stretching away on either side of the portico were the two wings of the building, not quite so high, with five windows in each. The view at the front was over a courtyard surrounded by handsome iron railings, and at the back of the white house lay the garden, in which flowers of every kind grew in the shade of the trees. I went running in search of the densest thickets and the most hidden paths, then sank onto a stone seat or rough wooden bench, and thought to myself, 'Here, she and I shall read together, exchanging a kiss between one page and the next.' Or, 'I shall take my easel and she her embroidery, and as we work, our talk will be of love, age-old but ever new!'

The good old caretaker and landlord's agent followed after me as best he could, calling out, 'Young man, a little more slowly, please. Look at that tree. Look at those plants. Look at the wonderful jet of water from this fountain. Come and see the amazing stalactites in this cave.'

I let him talk, and just carried on. But there was no way of avoiding it: I had to be good enough to enter the cave and admire the stalactites, since the old man had apparently staked all of his pride on what he had said.

The house was as clean and quiet inside as outside. 'This will be Carlotta's bedroom,' I said, entering a room with a cheerful, blue, floral-patterned wallpaper. There were two windows looking out over the garden and a big french-window on the side: from this room, you could surely see the sun rise and set. It also had an adjoining Turkish-style bathroom, with stained-glass windows that gave the light a quality of sensual unreality; and at the far end, behind a curtain, was the bathtub.

'There isn't a jasmin pergola here?' I asked the old man.

'There is,' he replied. 'And if you had only followed me slowly and attentively, I would have pointed it out to you.'

Then, throwing wide open the outside door of the room that I already decided should be Carlotta's, he ushered me into an elegant and secluded pergola, framed out of delicately scented summer jasmin. I picked one of the soft, white flowers and put it in my wallet, intending to give it to Carlotta when I told her I had found our love-nest. Within a few minutes the contract had been settled and the deposit paid.

'Until the day after tomorrow,' I called out to the caretaker as I climbed into the carriage.

'Don't worry, I'll be here waiting for you,' he replied with a deep bow.

And the horse set off at an exuberant trot, while the coachman, merrily cracking his whip, sang some crazy song, and I filled my lungs with air, my chest swelling with joy.

IV

When I got back to the inn at Mödling I found a letter from Carlotta. It read as follows:

'My Beloved,
Come home, for pity's sake! Come home at once! If you haven't found the villa, take me with you anyway. We'll stay at the inn together for a few days, and leave most of our things behind in Vienna in the meantime. If you only knew how sad and frightened I feel when I can't cling to your arm! I need you to laugh at my silly turns. I need to hear you scold me sweetly, and sometimes even a little crossly, for these dismal fancies that from time to time torment my mind. I need you to clasp me tightly to your chest and say to me, "Baby!" Then I feel ashamed of myself and pull myself together.

You know everything about me, save how trivial the cause that has given rise to my fears. I shall steel myself to write of it: but promise me never to speak of what sometimes oppresses me, since I want to love you with a carefree heart and with a smile on my lips – not that I need to ask you this, you're so good and generous to me. Five days ago, in the Prater that evening, I promised to tell you why I clung to you, trembling, when a tall, thin man passed in front of the bench where we were sitting. But sensing that it would upset me to talk about it, you didn't mention it again. You were content to believe that the man had never done me any harm, never tried to make any advances, never spoken to me before: and that is the truth.

However, one evening five months ago, before I came to live with you, I went with two of my girlfriends and two friends of theirs to the Diana-Saal. That huge beer-hall was so crowded downstairs that it was impossible to find anywhere to sit. We went upstairs – you know what it's like there, with a gallery running all the way round the hall and very large stalls, like separate compartments, opening on to it. Every table was taken. We had already gone almost full circle, slowly and without success, when I saw a lot of young men turn to look at me as we passed one of the stalls, and one fellow, in order to get a better look, had risen to his feet. You know how women have that ability to notice everything in a flash, without seeming to, out of the corner of their eyes. That young man's appearance struck me as sinister. His eyes were hidden by the lenses of his spectacles, and his flaxen hair came down to his shoulders; but that youthful face looked to me like the face of a dead man (I'm shuddering now!) – a dead man saying, "I love you." He spoke a few words to his friends, but I only caught a murmur. Meanwhile, the people sitting in the next compartment got up to leave, and we took their places.

One of the men with us had also noticed the fair-haired young fellow as we passed, and since he knew him by sight, he told us that it was Professor Gulz (I'm trembling, but I want to tell you the whole story), a famous scientist who spent his whole time, night and day, with corpses. I've always been squeamish, ever since I was a child, and I felt my blood run cold. Yet the orchestra went on with the waltz it was playing. All of a sudden, trumpets and drums gave way to some quieter bars of music, and then a voice,

Gulz's voice, reached my ears. He spoke these words in impassioned tones: "I swear to you, my friends, I swear by a presentiment that I have, and in the name of Science, that the lovely Carlotta" (how was it that he knew my name?) "will end up lying on my marble slab and reveal to my knife the secret of her beauty." The music became louder again, but in any case I should not have been able to hear anything more, I was so distressed. I begged that we should leave, and we did, going out in the opposite direction from where Gulz and his friends were – they could have had no idea that we were sitting so close, separated only by a low, thin partition.

This incident, I confess, left me with a profound fear of death; an immense horror of corpses; a deep-rooted, truly pathological sensitivity to anything connected, however remotely, with such morbid thoughts. That is why I trembled when I saw Gulz again. Oh God, if that dreadful man's oath were to come true! Come back, come back at once, my Beloved. Make me frivolous and carefree and reckless once more. I've such need for laughter and love. There, in the valley, beneath a jasmin pergola, in a beautiful country house, we'll both be happy. And then I'll be cured of this silliness and never again shall I rob you of even a quarter of an hour's joy, and I'll be for ever and always "the flighty young lady of the flowery fields".

It's already almost ten in the morning. I want to go and post this letter, and then I want to go for a walk by myself, in this lovely sunshine, up along the Danube. Come home, I implore you, come and hold me your arms tomorrow.

Your Arethusa'

I could not leave that same evening, since the last train for Vienna had already gone, but I told the maid to wake me very early the next day. At five o'clock I was in the railway carriage, looking straight into the sun, veiled in a light mist as it rose behind a thicket of trees, casting upon the meadows, hills and mountains the gentle warmth of its light. As the train sped along, I watched the sky, observing the rapid changes in its delicate, transparent colours, like those of a vast prism, in which every hue blended into the next with the softest of shadings not to be found in any palette.

Carlotta's letter had given me a rather disturbed night. I had the strangest nightmares, in which Karl Gulz kept reappearing in various, horribly fantastic guises. I did not sleep much. But when I got out of bed and opened the windows, all these ugly thoughts vanished. I reasoned to myself in the following manner: Like all men who spend most of the time alone, studying, Gulz needs to expound the ideas and feelings that accumulate inside him during those long hours of solitude – especially as he spends them with the dead. Inevitably, these ideas and feelings, maturing in an anatomist's operating theatre, must have a tendency to be unwholesome, gruesome, inhuman. Moreover, anyone used to doing what he will with inanimate things is inclined to believe that he should also have his own way on those rare occasions when he deals with the living. Added to which, Gulz might have drunk a few more glasses than usual. So his absurd oath – absurd because even if Carlotta were to die in Vienna, he would not be able to gain possession of her body – should not be taken seriously. In any case, Carlotta was the very picture of health. And besides, had Carlotta properly understood what Gulz had said, or rather, had she not unintentionally twisted his words to match the fears already in her mind? In short, partly by virtue of this reasoning, partly because I was already accustomed to Carlotta's innocent foibles, I was incapable of thinking of anything but the happiness of our forthcoming idyll in the white villa and shaded garden of Teufelsmühle.

At Perchtoldsdorf station, the train I was travelling in met the one coming from Vienna, which was carrying the post and newspapers. A news-vendor began to shout at the top of his voice: '*Wiener Zeitung, Presse, Wanderer, Ost-deutsche Post, Morgenpost, Vaterland, Glocke* – all the morning papers, sirs, straight off the press!' And he repeated the litany all over again. Some people bought this paper, and some bought that. I asked for the *Glocke*, because I knew that it was very prompt in reporting on the works on show in the Exhibition and I was, after all, very curious to know what impression my painting had made on the public over the last two days.

Under the heading 'Fine Arts', I found an article in which the most fulsome praise was lavished on my artistic skill. The critic expounded in great detail on my brush-stroke and palette, detecting in them all kinds of lofty, aesthetic, philosophical and moral qualities. He demonstrated that Arethusa's body, being of such perfection that Nature could not have created the like, must have been composed as bees make honey from flowers, or as Zeusi used the five young maidens of Croton to paint his Helen. Then followed a dissertation on the Ideal. He compared me a little with Correggio, Veronese, and Rubens, and a great deal with Minerva who emerged from Jove's brain fully armed. He concluded thus: 'We must end this encomium with an expression of regret. After being exposed to the avid viewing of the public and of artists and critics for only two days, this excellent work was bought today, as the gallery closed, and removed from the Exhibition. We do not know the name of the happy purchaser, but we hope that he will satisfy an honest curiosity, and return the work to the Exhibition for a few days more. The fault lies entirely with the Society's rules, which do not specify a minimum period for which a work must remain on show. This is not the first time that we have said this, but let us hope that this latest deplorable instance finally serves to open the eyes of the society's honourable administrators.'

The article was no masterpiece of criticism and style, but vanity is so eager to be flattered that I was very pleased. The trees along the route seemed to me extremely slow in passing, so impatient was I to show Carlotta the praises we had received, and to tell her that once we were in the country we would soon be working on another painting, ten times more beautiful than Arethusa. My thoughts went back to the ideas for paintings that had already occurred to me, while my hands turned the pages of the newspaper and my eyes strayed over the characters printed upon them. So, almost without taking anything in, I skimmed through some political news stories, then a few odd items reported lower down the page in the 'Local News' section. This was among them:

'ACCIDENT. At about ten thirty this morning, the funeral of the Contessina von Bardach, who has died at the age of twenty, was marked by one those misadventures that unfortunately we are obliged to lament almost daily. The coffin was covered with a white pall and garlanded with fresh flowers. The Contessina's young friends followed the hearse on foot, and behind them came the long line of carriages with relatives and family friends. The funeral procession, which had taken the road along the Danube to the Nussdorf cemetery, was just passing the Rossauer Lände, where the road narrows and the river has no parapet, when a woman, in her haste to step back, fell into the water and was carried a hundred metres downstream before she could be rescued. She was pulled unconscious from the river. And since no indication of her name or address were found, she was taken straight to the General Hospital. We have no further information. She is said to have been young and beautiful.'

I had read this item casually, but the last sentence arrested my attention. I reread it from the beginning. Every word seemed to blaze before me. My head felt as if it were on fire. I took Carlotta's letter from my wallet. I compared the date of the letter with that of the 'Local News' story: they were the same. The paper reported that the incident had occurred around ten thirty in the morning, and the letter said: 'It's already almost ten in the morning, I want to go and post this letter, and then I want to go for a walk by myself, up along the Danube.' And the incident had taken place along the Danube, upstream. And then there was her fear of death, her phobia, her invincible horror of funerals. And the victim's youth. And beauty. Everything reinforced the terrible apprehension in my mind. In vain I sought and prayed for a reason that would free me of the dreadful certainty already wringing my heart and choking me. I begged the people who had bought other newspapers to let me glance through them for a moment. One gentleman was slow in giving me his; I snatched it from his hand. He said nothing – I think he thought I was mad. The *Morgenpost* merely reported the story in the same words as the *Glocke*. The others did not mention it at all. In the meantime, we had arrived at Liesing. I leapt out and implored the stationmaster to send at once, to Dr Herzfeld's address, a telegram in which I told my friend to hurry to the South station to meet me. When I got back to my compartment, I found it empty. Apparently my travelling companions, not feeling too sure about me, had changed carriages. I do not know what I did. I only remember gripping on to the bars of the luggage rack, close to the ceiling, and straining my arms until I heard them crack.

At last we arrived at the South station, where Herzfeld was waiting for me. I took him by the arm and, dragging him after me, rushed him out of the station.

'Have you any news of Carlotta?'

'No.'

'You haven't see her today, or yesterday?'

'No. I never have any occasion to see her. And you yourself told me that she has no liking for doctors.'

'Do you know anything about a woman who fell into the Danube yesterday morning and was taken to the General Hospital?'

'Nothing at all.'

I reached the height of exasperation. I squeezed my friend's wrist so hard that he broke free, shouting with annoyance, 'Damn it, you're hurting me. Have you gone mad?' I apologized, and since we had meanwhile climbed into a two-horse carriage, which was taking us almost at a gallop to my lodgings on Franz-Josefs-Quai, I handed Herzfeld Carlotta's letter, together with the newspaper, pointing out to him how the letter ended, the relevant article, and the date on both of them. I stared at him.

He turned pale, but at once recovering himself, he said, 'It's a strange coincidence, but Carlotta is not the only young woman in Vienna, nor the only beautiful one, and she certainly isn't the only one who walked along the Danube yesterday morning.'

'But what about her dread of funerals?'

'And how do you know that the poor woman stepped back in fear? And in any case, unconsciousness and death are two different things. And by now that woman is probably suffering no more than the memory of having got wet.'

These words planted a seed of hope in me. Noticing this, and wanting to distract me, my friend went on, 'Besides, I've some good news for you, and three thousand florins that come with it. Your painting . . .'

'I know, it's been bought.' I cut him short with a gesture of annoyed indifference.

'It's been bought, and with no argument about the price. Yesterday evening the Director of the Society handed the money over to me, as your representative. I gave him a receipt for it. And here it is – three thousand florins, which I brought with me, thinking, when I received the telegram, that you might be in need of them.'

'You keep them for now, please.'

'No, no, take them.'

And I did, stuffing the bundle of notes into the breast pocket of my suit.

'Who bought the picture?' I added.

'No one knows.'

'What do you mean, no one knows?'

'That's what the Director told me. The buyer didn't leave his name, and he had the painting taken away by his own porters, without a moment's delay.'

As we approached Franz Josefs-Quai, I felt my fever of impatience growing. The carriage stopped outside my house.

'Signora Carlotta?' I asked the caretaker in a voice choked with fearful anxiety. A flicker of joy went through me at the sight of the man's placid face.

He replied calmly, 'I haven't seen her since yesterday morning. I assumed that the young lady had gone to join you in the country.'

'To the General Hospital, quickly,' I shouted to the coachman, 'quickly, at full speed.'

My friend tried to comfort me. But by now I was overcome with despair and no longer listening to him. However, he insisted that I promise to behave reasonably, to stay close to him, on no account to talk to anybody, and to leave everything to him, since he knew his way around the hospital and was no stranger to the doctors and nurses.

V

Eight or nine orderlies, in their pale-green, wax-canvas gowns, which came down to their ankles and were buttoned up to the chin, were seated in the lobby, chatting. The main entrance, at the far end of the lobby, was closed. We went up three steps, through a door to the left of the wooden gate, and as we opened it a bell rang, with a loud silvery sound that made me jump.

My earlier state of overwrought despair had given way to a sinister, almost cynical calm. I observed myself as though I were another person. My mind focused with dispassionate attention on the most insignificant details: I remember that, while Herzfeld searched through the enormous hospital register, I stared at a patch of damp on the room's bare wall, and somehow detecting in it the forms of fighting men, I was reminded of Leonardo da Vinci.

Nevertheless, I heard Herzfeld remark to a doctor on duty, 'I can't find in the register under "Admissions" any mention of a young woman who was pulled out of the Danube yesterday and, according to the newspapers, brought to this hospital around eleven in the morning.'

'It could be that the papers published a complete yarn,' replied the doctor. 'They publish so many! Have you looked under "Discharges"?'

'Yes.'

'Is she there?'

'No, she isn't.'

'That certainly means, then, that if she came in, she hasn't left, or at least that she didn't leave the place alive. But anyway she might well be here. Sometimes, in urgent cases, the patients are taken straight to the wards, and that fool of a porter forgets to register them.'

'Let's go to the wards then,' Herzfeld said to me.

I followed him. We came into a huge quadrangle, with colonnades all the way round, planted with lots of fine trees. The tops of the trees stood out against the white rendering of the floor above. Lined up on one side were at least thirty stretchers, all folded away in their dingy blue testers with a white dove at one end. We entered a very long ward on the ground floor. The small high windows opening onto the arcade did not let in much light and must have been of little use for ventilation, because as we came through the door I felt my throat contract at the horrid stench.

My friend said to me, 'You must look carefully. The nurses, Sisters of Charity, and the doctors work in shifts; we can't rely on their information.'

Then began our sorry search. Herzfeld and I examined those patients' faces one by one – thin, white faces, with dull, sunken eyes, and colourless lips. None complained. The facial convulsions of some betrayed their acute internal pain. Others seemed to suffer not so much bodily pain as mental anguish. And there were those, humming to themselves, who showed how tenacious hope can be. One woman was asleep: we went up to the top of the bed and, gently lifting the sheet, uncovered her gaunt face.

And so we went through the second ward, the third, the fourth, and goodness knows how many others, until we emerged into the big quadrangle again, at the far end of another side of the portico, and came into a second, smaller courtyard, also planted with trees, then into a third, where we climbed up a wide staircase to the first-floor loggia. Herzfeld stopped frequently to talk to the attendants and doctors.

I did not hear what they said, but I saw that they answered my friend's questions with negative gestures or by shaking their heads, as though saying, 'We know nothing about it.' My heart-beat was regular, but when I put my hand to my forehead it was wet with perspiration.

'Another thirty rooms to check,' said Herzfeld. 'We've already seen about five hundred patients,' he added. 'There are at least another seven hundred.'

The wards on the first floor had higher ceilings, were airier and lighter; the beds seemed cleaner and the patients less sad. In the tubercular ward, there was hardly any coughing to be heard. The patients were nearly all young women, and nearly all of them beautiful. One looked like an angel. She was sitting in bed, covered up to her hips with a blanket. Her clean night-dress, buttoned at the collar and at the wrists, fell in small straight pleats over her thin chest; her arms lay on either side of her, and her hands, with their palms turned up, were white and shapely. Her brown hair was spread on the broad pillow, framing her extremely pale face – a face that Fra Angelico would have drawn with a sigh; and from that drawing Donatello would have modelled in pure alabaster those lovely, wan cheeks, that fine chin and clear brow, those thin lips and that somewhat aquiline nose. Her eyes were fixed, with a direct, level gaze, on something beyond the wall of the room, perhaps beyond this earth. A ray of sunshine, entering through the nearby window and falling on the sheets, cast a reflected light on that calm face, which seemed to me encircled with a halo. We had not noticed a man sitting beside the bed, with his face buried in his hands, and his head resting on the blanket. At the sound of our footsteps, he stood up. He was a white-haired, emaciated old fellow. Tears sprang from his eyes and his breathing was broken with sobs. As we passed by, he whispered to us in a tone of dreadful desperation, 'She's my daughter!'

We went through that ward, then another, and yet another, and on and on. My body was exhausted, my limbs were trembling, but my mind, still alert, observed everything, noticed everything, with the kind of concentration, at once intense and abstracted, that some-times follows or accompanies great emotional disturbances. Three times, at three beds where, you could tell, the long shape of what was already a corpse lay covered with a brown blanket, Herzfeld stopped to read the cards with the patient's details recorded on them.

There remained only the patients in the surgical wards to visit — there my ears were assailed for the first time by high-pitched screams — and in the clinical wards, where the professors were just then giving instruction to students at the bedsides. Old Grun was standing beside one woman, pointing out to about a dozen young men goodness knows what notable scientific case. The poor woman had raised her arms and crossed them over her face to hide, while the professor's slow voice droned on. A brief and unclear glimpse of the arms, shoulders and bosom of that woman, who had a splendid figure, suddenly made me see red. I was about to rush towards the bed in a fury, when the beautiful patient, startled by the touch of Grun's hand, turned her head so that her long hair — black as a raven's wing — came tumbling down on the side. I instantly calmed down. 'Better dead,' I thought.

'We're done with the living,' Herzfeld said to me as we came out of that last ward. 'Let's go downstairs.'

We went back through the loggia wards, then down the staircase we had ascended, across the courtyards, and along the porticos, making for another corner of the large quad-rangle. We walked straight through the part of the building reserved for men and came to the Observation Room, situated at the back of that vast area. In a huge, well-lit room were perhaps twenty beds, only five or six of them occupied by corpses, which science had not yet entirely relinquished to death. Tied to their hands and feet were four pieces of string leading to the next room, where guards kept watch night and day over the numbered bells to which the string was attached. The corpses were all male.

As we came into a final courtyard, which was low-built and deserted, Herzfeld said to me, 'Wait for me here. I won't be more than minutes.' And he disappeared.

I was left on my own. Walking down the side with the sun beating down on it, I saw lizards hiding among the nettles. I came to a door with a sign saying, 'Mortuary'. I went inside. The door slammed shut behind me with a great bang. The place was dark and empty. It was like a long corridor and, closed, at the far end was a big, heavy door with space above it for the only, fan-shaped window. The damp, brown, stone walls glistened, reflecting the dim, distant light; the floor was wet. I went up to the door and tried unsuccessfully to open it. As I turned back, I thought I discerned some whitish patches on the floor in the corner, by the door through which I had entered. I went up to them and saw that they were corpses. As I grew accustomed to the dark, I gradually began to distinguish their shapes. Three children lay side by side, as though trying to keep warm. Next was a line of six men, all of them naked, purple, stripped of flesh, with their eyes open. Then came five white crosses. I looked closer: these crosses lay upon five black sheets that were covering something. Taking care where I put my feet, I lowered my face right down next to them and, holding my breath, lifted the top edge of the first blanket to reveal the face and shoulders of a naked woman. After I had similarly examined the second, third, fourth and last – 'She's not here,' I cried with joy, 'she's not here.' And I was about to make my escape. But having tried in vain to lift the big latch on the door that opened onto the courtyard, and seeing another door, over in the corner, which was open, I went out that way, into a corridor leading to a big room some yards further along.

The light dazzled me. A line of narrow, white marble tables, with rounded edges and a raised rim all the way round, stood beneath the large windows. Most were empty, but on two of them were stretched out two men: one, an old man, who looked pleased not to be alive any more; the other, young, with shining black hair, parted lips revealing the whiteness of his teeth, and a broad, high forehead that seemed still full of thoughts. The instruments required for an autopsy glinted on the tables beside the two bodies.

Herzfeld, who had entered without my noticing, threw his arms round my neck and exclaimed, 'Thank heavens. There you are, at last. I didn't know where you'd got to. I was worried about you.'

'Well?'

'She's not here, and she's not in the deaths register.'

'So she wasn't admitted, and as far we know she hasn't left the place, one way or another. And she's nowhere to be found!'

'The newspapers must have been lying. Your caretaker was probably right. She was probably impatient to see you again and set off on her own, and is now waiting for you at Mödling.'

The blood started to flow through my veins again, new life returned to my limbs, and I felt a new strength, overwhelming and joyful, stirring within me. A moment before, I had been feeling utterly bowed down and dwarf-ish. Now I straightened up and thought myself a giant. Hope came hurtling into the hollow emptiness of my mind like a seething torrent crashing down from a great height. There was within me a confusion of renascent joys, of rekindled desires. Love, pleasure, nature, art and glory sang in my heart in a divine tumult. The scent of jasmine caressed my nostrils and I thought again with fervid delight of the white villa in the Brühl Valley.

Grabbing my good friend Herzfeld by the arm, I cried, 'Let's get out of this hellish place.'

And I raced off like a mad child. I was already about to leave the building and step outside, when I saw these words written in big black letters on a nearby door: KARL GULZ'S LABORATORY.

VI

The door was open. I rushed into the room. There, in the middle, on a marble slab, was Carlotta's body.

'Carlotta! Carlotta!' I yelled, throwing myself upon her, and impetuously bringing my face close to hers. Two impassive eyes stared into mine: I felt a shudder run through me. I wanted to place a kiss on that brow, I wanted to carry away that body, but a terrible force repelled me. I recoiled, trembling. I collapsed onto a chair and murmured to myself, 'There's nothing! Nothing left!'

Herzfeld came up to me, alarmed. 'For pity's sake,' he said, trying to drag me out, 'let's get away from here.'

A moment later I blacked out. For some time – maybe an hour, or two – I remained utterly dead to the world. I dreamed. Everything that had happened swirled around me as though in a thick fog, taking on the appearance of some dreadful and deathly phantasmagoria. It was a frightening faint. A long procession of menacing clouds and ugly memories passed before me. I was scared out of my wits. I thought I was drowning in nothingness. I felt two cold lips biting me on the cheek, and two arms, two scrawny arms, two bones, strangling me in a monstrous embrace. I tried to cry out. My voice died in my throat.

Then I opened my eyes again, and I could still see the corpse's fixed, impassive eyes.

My heart was torn with anguish, and I was assailed again with horrid visions of worms and shin-bones. And these skeletons stood upright and these worms became enormous, and they began to sway together in a diabolical dance. I laughed.

'What are you laughing at?' asked poor Herzfeld, holding my head, bathing my forehead with ice-cold water, and giving me goodness knows what acrid-smelling stuff to sniff.

'I'm not going mad,' I replied, 'unfortunately I'm not going mad. Leave me here. I want to talk to the Doctor.'

Gulz, whom I had not seen, then gravely stepped forward, and stood beside the corpse. 'Where everything ends for you,' he said, 'for us, everything begins. Death is life.'

Had I encountered this man not long before, I would have seized him by the neck and throttled him. Now I looked at him with despairing resignation.

'This time,' he went on, 'fate has been willing to help me, and without any of my doing one of my most ardent desires has been fulfilled. I'm sorry,' he added after a pause, turning to me, 'I'm sorry for your sake; but I'm glad for science.'

'Swear to God that you will not defile those limbs,' I exclaimed, rising to my feet, and making a supreme effort to revive a little passion in my heart and voice.

'Feel how cold they are,' the Doctor continued. 'Feel, they're more chilly than the steel instruments I have in my hand. The lovely pinkness of these limbs doesn't come from the redness of the blood, but from a coloured liquid injected into the tissues. I have rediscovered Ruysch of Leiden's secret. And my specimens excel those of the Amsterdam Museum. Please take a look around you.'

I looked. The room was lined with vases of all sizes, filled with anatomical specimens, and glass-cases containing embalmed bodies that appeared to be alive. Over the cupboards were a great many unframed paintings hanging on the walls. Among them, I noticed one of someone I knew, painted by Raal: it was a portrait of a poor old man who had posed as a model for me, for my first life-studies, and whom I had been very fond of. He had died two years ago; but there in the glass-case, beneath his portrait, he seemed to be breathing. His long, silvery beard fell over his broad chest, and running vertically across the lines on his tranquil brow was a thick scar, which had given the good old man countless opportunties to tell of battles that had taken place half a century earlier. Raal could well have copied the vital figure in his painting from such a mummy, so true to life were its colouring and features, and even its facial expression, not only in terms of the person's physical aspect, but also his moral character.

'This,' Gulz went on in a slow voice, 'is only a part, the superficial part, of my studies. In this, I need the artist to help me, to remind me of the appearance of life. But appearance is only formal: I seek to find how it is determined by matter. As Man's bones, entrails, and tissues explain life, so they explain beauty. Art embraces science. You know, sir, that the right auricle of the heart is the last part of the human body to cease functioning. The time will come, I swear, when physiology and psychology will form a single discipline. Not only will I die before this union takes place, but so will many more generations depart this world. Nevertheless, it will take place. And, for myself, I should be happy if I could in some way aid this great discovery – a discovery that will finally reveal what men have been seeking for thousands upon thousands of years: the explanation of their being, the material substance and the workings of their thoughts and feelings.'

'There's the material substance,' I said, in a tone of grim irony, pointing to Carlotta's corpse.

'Do you think a tree has a soul? And does it not live, and die? What is it that makes it live? Certain special activities of certain molecules. The life of a leaf and the life of Schiller's mind differ only in degree. The essence is the same. The mystery of vegetal life has been discovered; so, too, will that of animal life be discovered, and ultimately of intelligent life. But how many years is it since we've known with certainty how plants live and die? For how many centuries before that was this easy problem ineffectually investigated? Are we to tell ourselves now that the book of Nature is closed? On the contrary, it is more open to us today than ever before. And men will read it all, to the very last page.'

While the Doctor spoke, I kept my eyes fixed upon the corpse, with its arms lying straight by its sides, the hands resting upturned on the marble, legs together, head tilted back a little, mouth half-open, eyes staring, hair hanging down over centre of the far end of the table: a vain symmetry, lugubrious and chilling. This body meant nothing to me any more.

'Think, sir,' Gulz continued, 'think what remains of your passion. Had you loved a spirit, you would love her still, if only in memory. But you loved a fleeting manifestation of matter, and it's natural that, when the object of passion changes form, passion should die. Yet I love this body a thousand times more now than before. inasmuch as it helps to bring me closer to the truth. In a word, the only concrete thing, the only real thing, is science. The rest is illusion or fantasy.'

I had felt crushed. These harsh and at the same impassioned words, both bland and sinister, subdued me. No light dawned in my mind, but a deep and dismal calm entered my heart. Looking round, I saw my picture of Arethusa, still on the floor, leaning against the wall.

'I'd like to buy back that painting, Doctor,' I murmured, drawing from my pocket the money that Herzfeld had handed over to me that morning, and which I had not touched.

'Very well. My memory will suffice now,' replied Gulz with a sigh, and he offered me his hand. Heaven knows why, I shook it. And having cast a final glance at Carlotta's body, I very slowly left the room, leaning on Herzfeld's arm.

As we crossed the bridge over the Danube I took out of my wallet the jasmine flower I had picked the previous day in the pergola of the house in Teufelsmühle, and stopping by the parapet, I let it drop.

After a moment the white speck had disappeared in the dark green waters.

CHRISTMAS EVE

This is my poor Giorgio's manuscript: the Giorgio that I taught to read, and write, and so many other fine things. And often, as a child, he would stand on one side of me, and poor Emilia on the other, and they would smother me with kisses. I remember that one day Emilia suddenly said to me, 'Maria, you've a white hair!' And she tried to pull it out. My hair was my greatest pride. Twenty years later, Giorgetta, who is now in heaven, was sitting on my lap, and she said to me in the same voice and with the same wonder as her mother, 'Maria, you've a black hair!' And she pulled a face, because she liked these snow-white curls of mine.

There is nothing about my Giorgio that I do not love. But this manuscript, which I don't much understand, wrings my heart and makes me weep. I find no peace except in church, praying to God. I would have given my own good health, my life, to see those three dear children, who are no longer with me, well and happy.

Signor Giorgio's manuscript

I had been suffering terrible stomach pains for several days. I could not eat. I had been dining alone at the Cavour Inn that evening, and I had to leave the table after the soup. The room was cold and virtually empty. There were three Germans, sighing at every mouthful, and a Frenchman, in despair at not knowing whom to bore to death, chatted desultorily with the waiters, saying that for him there had never been any such thing as Easter, or Christmas, or New Year's Day, or any other women's foolishness or childish nonsense. Then, happy to have solemnly professed his strength and freedom of spirit, he stuck his snout into his plate.

In the street, the reddish, almost dark glow of the

streetlamps could be picked out, one by one. But the very thick fog was suffused with a pale whitish glimmer, both brighter and denser around the lamps, by which it was barely possible to discern a stretch of shining wet pavement, the dim shadow of a person who bumped into you in passing, the indistinct shape of a carriage driving by, cautiously and soundlessly. Otherwise, the streets, usually so full of people and vehicles, were almost deserted: the silence seemed full of pitfalls. Everything became vast and mysterious. You lost your bearings. You suddenly found yourself at the corner of a street that you thought was still some distance ahead, or you assumed you had reached a crossing that was further on. You sought your way through the mist, soaked through, stiff with cold, suspecting that you had turned deaf and blind.

I stumbled on the steps projecting from the church of San Francesco, and a woman's cry emerged from the thick fog. Then a ragged child came running between my legs, begging for money, and wishing me a Merry Christmas, or some such thing. I pushed him aside. I gave him nothing. He persisted. I threatened him. I was in an ugly state of mind. In the Galleria, a reeling drunkard was singing some tedious old song. Under the portico in the Piazza del Duomo, there were two police officers walking along slowly, with measured steps.

In the narrow streets beyond Piazza Mercanti, the fog, trapped between the tall houses, had thinned a little. You could see that all the shops were shut, even the inns had their doors closed. But high-spirited sounds of merriment emerged from windows here and there. Happiness reigned in every dining-room. I heard the clinking of glasses, shrieks of joy, loud choruses of vulgar, shameless laughter. It was an orgy – but the blessed orgy of the family. I stopped to listen beneath one of the noisiest balconies. At first I could make out nothing at all, then gradually I managed to distinguish voices amid the great clatter of plates and glasses. A child was shouting, 'Mama, another slice of panettone.' Someone else was clamouring, 'Papa, another drop of wine.' And I could tell what the mother and father were saying, and I could just see the jovial grandfather and smiling grandmother. I pulled up the collar of my coat over my ears.

I did not know what to do. The streets were like a graveyard, the theatres were all closed; owing to the Christmas holiday there were no newspapers. I was all by myself, alone in Milan, where I had no friends, male or female, no acquaintances: alone in the world. This time a year ago, on Christmas Day, after lunch in the handsome dining-room of our house in Via di Po, I had been down on the carpet, with Giorgetta and her little friends making me give them horse-rides, climbing on my back and using the whip. And Emilia chided me, 'Really, Giorgi, shame on you: playing with children at the age of twenty-three.' And she said to Giorgetta, 'Leave your uncle in peace.' But the children, taking no notice, continued to dance round me, and to deafen me with their cries. I then got to my feet and picked them up in my arms, one at a time, giving them the last of the sugared almonds and a kiss on the cheek.

What happiness! Such happiness!

The walk and the fog had given my body a great hunger that frightened me. The immoderate and indiscriminate amounts of pepsin that I had taken in the last few days, which had not achieved anything except to make the excruciating pains in my stomach worse than ever, were probably doing what they were supposed to all of a sudden, and stimulating gastric activity. I felt as if I could devour an ox, but unfortunately I had long grown accustomed to the dreadful tricks of the pylorus. And yet that evening I had a restless desire to have a good time. Even the grief that usually overwhelmed me completely, allowing no opportunity for boredom, gave way to yawns. For the first time in a month – since my beloved Emilia had placed her hand, already cold, on my hair, while I hid my tears in her pillow; since I had fled from Turin and gone wandering from place to place through Italy – I felt the want of some distraction, the need to talk to someone, to open my heart to a friend, a woman, or a doctor, and to tell of my moral anguish, and physical agony. A renewed selfishness grew within me. I regretted not being in Turin, where I would have dined, and chatted and wept, with kind-hearted Maria. A little before it was time to go to bed, she would have whispered to me, in that very meek voice of hers, 'Signor Giorgio, for pity's sake, have a little faith. Listen: do your old nurse a kindness, say the rosary with me. Go on, be a good fellow: it won't take long. Then, you'll see, God and the Madonna will instil a great resignation into your heart, and you will gradually be filled with the peace and comfort of the just. Giorgetta and Signora Emilia are praying for you. You could get closer to them by praying a little, too, Signor Giorgio.' And to see the face of that woman who is almost a mother to me smile with sublime gratification, I should probably have done as Emilia used to do; I should have knelt and said the rosary responses.

I found myself near the Biblioteca Ambrosiana. Whenever I walked without knowing where I was going – and this was something that was always happening to me – my legs would carry me to the streets in that vicinity. In one of these streets lived a shop girl that I had noticed on the second day of my brief stay in Milan. Afterwards, I had gone back to see her three or four times, virtually every evening in fact, at about five thirty: the time of day when it is already dark and the streetlights come on; when the toing and froing of people hurrying home for dinner, and the coming and going of carriages, cast a certain busy impatience even upon the quiet stroller, thrilling his imagination.

I feel a deep shame in confessing it, but this milliner had attracted me because of her resemblance to Emilia. My grief was heightened by a vague sense of remorse. By seeking out and studying – as instinct irresistibly compelled me – certain minute and fleeting similarities between my beloved Emilia's appearance and that of the women I met, and even photographs that I saw, I felt I was profaning her sacred memory. And all too often I was then forced to acknowledge that these resemblances existed only in my imagination. The number of times I have stood for half-an-hour staring in a photographer's shop-window! And yet I had in my wallet four different portraits of Emilia, as well as three of Giorgetta that could have been three pictures of Emilia as a child. Nevertheless, during the five days I was in Florence, I remember having gone twice to the far end of the Corso di Porta Romana, even though it was raining, specially to look at an attractive little head in a picture-framer's shop, in among a great many stiff sergeants of the line and a great many ugly countrywomen all decked in frills; a head that I had seen for the first time when I happened to be making my way on foot to La Certosa, and which I would like to have bought, had shame not restrained me.

The girl was always hurrying about her·business, but the first time I encountered her was in front of the window of a big jeweller's shop, where she had stopped. The lights were coming on, and the gold pieces glinted, and the diamonds shone, and the pearls had a wonderful warm lustre. She suddenly turned, with sparkling eyes and lips parted in a joyful smile, revealing her extremely white teeth. Then, noticing me, she shrugged her shoulders and off she went, like a streak of lightning. I had difficulty keeping up with her, but she side-stepped carriages and slipped through the crowd unperturbed, holding the skirt of her cape a little off ground, and on and on she went, stepping briskly. At one turning I thought I had lost her, but there she was again, in the distance, passing in front of a café – and I went following after. And she turned right, and left, then suddenly disappeared.

The next day, as I waited for her in the street where I had lost sight of her, I saw her enter the doorway of a house. She was quickly swallowed up by the pitch-darkness of the entrance, then came the ring of a bell, and she was gone.

This girl's smile had thrown me into a state of great

turmoil. Emilia used to look at me like that when I brought her a fine present on my return from some trip. Or when, on my name-day and on certain anniversaries, she came into my bedroom early in the morning, having knocked lightly on the door and asked in that sweet voice of hers, 'May I come in?' Then she rushed up to me and fastened onto my tie a pin with a magnificent pearl (the one I always wear), or put a new chain for my watch round my neck, or slipped into my pocket a leather wallet decorated with a silver pattern that she had designed. Once, no more than two and a half years ago, although I didn't want her to pull off my boots, with those delicate pink hands of hers, she had insisted, replacing them with a pair of slippers she herself had embroidered – oh, so beautifully, so beautifully. Then I clasped those two hands and kissed her brow, which was radiant with joy. Then we heard a furious knocking at the door, fit to bring the house down: it was Giorgetta, who came in with a shower of kisses, gales of laughter, a whirl of happiness.

I had no hope of seeing my shop-girl that Christmas Eve, as it was long since past the usual time, and in any case she, like all other mortals, must have been busy with Christmas dinner festivities. And yet I went past the entrance to her house. It seemed to me that inside the dark doorway was a shadow. I strolled by, looked in, and glimpsed a woman's hat. The woman hurriedly hid herself. It was her. My heart was thumping. I remained uncertain for a moment whether I should continue on my way or turn back. In the end I retraced my steps, and once more, out of the corner of my eye, I saw the figure, standing there. I felt ashamed of myself, ashamed at the same time of my desire and my timidity. I went past again. I had never been able to address an unknown woman in the street, however little averse she appeared, without the greatest reluctance. And on the very rare occasions when I had done so, it was, above all else, the fear of appearing ridiculous that prompted me. But that evening my soul felt the need to unburden itself. For a month I had locked up inside me my grief, desires, and youth. I urged myself to be bold, and since the figure was standing practically on the doorstep, I greeted her.

'Good evening.'

She did not reply, indeed she took a few steps back, melting into the darkness. I was delighted. I would have been sorry if the girl had been too forward. But a moment later she stuck her head out of the doorway again, giving a quick glance to left and right.

I approached her once more, and said again, 'Good evening.'

She responded with a none too polite shrug of her shoulders, and said, 'Leave me alone. Get along with you!' And since I made no move to go, she added, 'You've no manners, and no call to be bothering an honest girl like me.'

Then my pride rebelled, making me turn away, and I resolutely went some hundred yards. Ten minutes later I was back at the doorway.

Striving to make my voice sound meek and ingratiating, I murmured, 'Are you waiting for someone? Perhaps I could keep you company! I'm a decent fellow, you know. And besides, you must have seen me on more than one occasion.'

'Certainly I have. You spend your time following me about. Evidently you've nothing else to do.'

'Nothing better, no, because I find you so attractive. What's your name?'

'It can't matter to you.'

'Indeed it does. I want to know at least what name I should address my sighs to.'

'Ah, you poor devil! Now, go away, at once. If my husband sees you . . .'

'So you're waiting for your husband?'

'Of course. He should have been here half an hour ago.'

And she stamped her feet in annoyance – perhaps, too, because of the cold, since her hands, which I had fleetingly touched, were frozen.

'It's that husband of yours who has no manners. And were you supposed to be going for a walk, if I might ask?'

'A walk! You must be joking! I was supposed to be going out to dinner.'

An idea occurred to me then, which I instantly seized upon, especially as I felt I had already been so gauche. 'To dinner? Come and have dinner with me.'

'Oh, I couldn't do that! No, no. And what if my husband were to find out?'

'He won't. We'll take a carriage and go to the Cavour Inn, we'll eat truffles and drink champagne, and have a good time.'

'But I don't know you.'

'After dinner, you'll see, we'll be old friends.'

She smiled the smile that had seduced me and made me shiver, then, with a very determined gesture, she exclaimed, 'Let's go.'

The room at the Cavour Inn, where I had been staying for several days, was very warm. The flames flickered in the hearth. I ordered two candelabras to be lit, as well as the lamp that hung from the ceiling. The walls, which were golden-yellow patterned with red flowers, looked garish in that bright light.

The imperious waiter eyed the girl from head to toe with grand disdain, and began to lay the table – a small, oval table standing by the fire, and which was very soon covered with all kinds of delicious things. My stomach was impatient: had it been cut open, as lambs' stomachs are in order to extract the pepsin, a rare abundance of gastric juices would have been found inside me. My appetite, my need to eat, was so great that it seemed to me impossible that I would not be able to digest. And my shop-girl had almost made me forget this treat for my stomach, a treat that I had so long yearned for in vain. She had already removed her hat, and thrown her muff on a seat and her cloak on an armchair, and she was standing in front of the mirror rearranging her hair. Holding her arms in an arc raised to her head clearly revealed the contours of her body, scantily clad in a close-fitting dress that was so light it looked like a summer dress. I sat her down beside me, without even glancing at her, and we began to swallow large oysters, and to drink good amber-coloured wine that put new life into me. The old, persistent and intolerable pains in my intestines had gone. I breathed again, I rejoiced. Oh God! At last I could eat. I had already exhausted all possible remedies many months ago – even, to my shame, those in the classified advertisement sections of the newspapers. I had consulted distinguished doctors from Berlin and Paris. And yet I had to survive on diluted broth, milk, coffee, little bits of undercooked meat. Epicurus! Epicurus! And I thought of the Emperor Tiberius, who gave his poet two hundred thousand sesterces for a dialogue in which mushrooms, the warbler, the oyster and the thrush disputed pre-eminence.

For my part, I would have awarded pre-eminence to the pheasant with truffles that my love and I ate in religious silence, quenching our thirst with sips of a superb claret. The assortment of glasses – on whose facets every candle cast a streak of brightness, like little electric sparks – kept growing in number. Stemmed, mug-shaped, large-bowled, long-necked – there were glasses of every shape and size, as well as the big stately water-glass, as yet unfilled. At every shake of the table, they vibrated and tinkled, scattering thousands of white sparks on the tablecloth. The wine was like liquefied precious stones: amethysts, rubies, topazes.

Having laid out the desserts on the table and uncorked the bottles of champagne, the waiter gave us a most respectful bow that was not without malice, and left the room.

'Would you not like anything else, my dear?'

'No, thank you, sir, I'm full.'

'A glass of champagne?'

'That, yes. I like it so much and I've drunk it only once in my life.'

'When?'

'One evening when two gentlemen took me to dinner at the Rebecchino. There was another girl there too.'

'And your husband?'

'What husband?'

'The one you were waiting for in the doorway this evening.'

'Ah, I'd forgotten about him. Damn him!'

'Don't you love him?'

'Me? I met him ten days ago, and he's married. I told you I was waiting for my husband so that you, being a gentleman, sir, as I thought, wouldn't think badly of me.'

'Let's drop the formality, shall we?'

'If you like.'

'Tell me, have you never been in love?'

'Let me see, now. Once, I think, but only for a few days. He was a man of forty, with a black moustache. He used to beat me and wanted me to get money for him. Of course, men are all the same. Here, let me tell you what happened . . .'

I was not listening to her any more. I was looking at her. She was ugly. Her trim figure was not bad, but she had coarse features, a rough complexion speckled with little yellow spots, greeny-coloured eyes, and fine parallel lines scoring her brow.

I cut in as she continued to tell me her adventures in a raucous voice, and amused herself by mixing together the various-coloured wines and then swilling down the foul concoction.

'How old are you?'

'Nineteen.'

And she resumed her story in a desultory fashion. She got up; she examined with curiosity the heavy gilt frames of the mirrors; she lay back in the armchairs, and on the sofa; she threw herself on the bed; she came up behind me to caress me with her rough hands; then she ate some sugared almonds, filled her pockets with them, drained a glass of champagne, and examined with curiosity, one by one, the objects on the chests of drawers and small tables.

She seized upon some pictures of Emilia, crying, 'Oh, I've found her, I've found her. She's your sweetheart!'

A burning shame and anger went rushing to my head, and I leapt to my feet.

'Give me those pictures.'

'Your darling, your darling.'

'Give me those pictures at once,' I repeated in a fury.

And she went running round the room, climbing onto the armchairs and holding the portraits up in the air, and stupidly kept on chanting, 'Your darling, your darling.'

Then I went into a blind rage. I chased after her, saying again and again in a strangled voice, 'Give me those pictures, you wretched woman.' And I snatched them from her hand, having squeezed her wrist so hard that she fell with a cry, onto a high-backed chair, virtually unconscious.

I was immediately at her side with some eau de Cologne. She soon recovered, although her arm and hand still hurt a little.

Ashamed of my brutal behaviour, I murmured, 'Forgive me. Forgive me.'

From the chest of drawers I took a watch that I had bought some days earlier, and I slipped the chain around her neck.

She carefully examined the watch, which was very small, and the chain, which was heavy, and continuing to examine them, completely appeased, she asked, 'Are they gold?'

'Certainly.'

She looked up, gazing into my face with her gleaming black eyes. And she smiled. In her delight, her face had taken on a new expression, with the curve of her parted, coral lips framing the pure whiteness of her perfect teeth. In fact she looked like Emilia.

'Do you forgive me?' I asked her.

She came rushing over and hugged me in her arms. Then she sat down on a low stool, stretching out her legs on the carpet, and laying her head on my lap. She tipped her head back: her hair, dishevelled and half loose, served her as a pillow. And, seated as I was in a big armchair, I bent over to look at her, and asked her to smile broadly.

To my great astonishment the wine I had drunk and the delicacies I had eaten (I should not be able to eat and drink as much again in a year) had had no adverse effect on my stomach. But they had, of course, worked upon my imagination. I was not drunk, since I can recall today in exact detail the most minute particulars of that night. But I was in a strange state of moral and physical excitement that, without diminishing my memory, robbed me of responsibility for my actions. I could have killed a man with a fruit-knife, just for fun.

The girl's teeth fascinated me.

'Why are you looking at me like that?'

'I was looking at your teeth.'

'Do you like them?'

'What do you do to keep them so shiny?'

'I don't do anything.'

They were all even, all set regularly, the upper ones a little larger and so thin they seemed transparent.

'A girlfriend of mine,' she added, 'the one that came with me to dinner at the Rebecchino with those two men, had a rotten tooth. You should have seen what a lovely tooth she had it replaced with. And you couldn't tell that it wasn't natural. It cost a lot, though: twenty lire! You can imagine, there are some days when I'd sell one of mine for twenty lire.'

'Give me one for five hundred.'

'Of course! I'd have it replaced and keep four hundred and eighty lire! Of course! Of course!' And she clapped her hands. 'But now tell me,' she went on, 'why were you ready to practically kill me for those pictures of yours? I wasn't going to eat them, you know.'

'Let's not talk about it. It's a sad story that upsets me.'

She looked abashed. She yawned, stretched her arms, settled her head more comfortably on my lap, and fell asleep.

Not wanting to wake the girl, I sat still and gradually became immersed in my painful cherished memories. Giorgetta, too, had frequently settled down to sleep on my lap, while her mother read to me in her clear voice an article from the newspaper, or a chapter of a novel. But my niece's hair was as fair as a saint's halo, her face like the face of an angel, and the breath that escaped her of the very purest, purer than the mountain breeze at sunrise. Occasionally, she would stir, talking in her dream to her doll. I would wait until she was sound asleep, and then very slowly I would get up, holding one arm under her back, supporting her little legs with the other, and I would carry her on tiptoe, followed by Emilia, to her beautiful golden cradle beneath the lace canopy her mother had embroidered. It was in that very same cot, which was so pretty, that Giorgietta died, choked by diphtheria. Before she was taken to heaven, she looked at us one by one – me, her mother and old Maria – with those darling blue eyes of hers, and could not understand why we were weeping. Even the doctor was weeping.

The rings under Emilia's eyes, which at the beginning were a delicate blue, turned to dark brown, and the soft rosiness of her cheeks changed to a pale ethereal shade of ivory. The sweetness of that gentle disposition, eager to do good, always forgetful of herself, innocent, kind and wise, was being purified into the nature of an angel.

As the illness gradually gnawed away at her entrails, her spirit rose up to God. In the final hours, when racked with excruciating pains, she tried to conceal them from everyone with countless sublime stratagems. When I very gently raised her head and arranged her pillows more comfortably, she whispered to me in a faint voice, 'I'm sorry, Giorgio. You see how much trouble I am to you!' And she tried to squeeze my hand. And to Maria and everyone else, for however small a service, she never stopped repeating with a smile, 'Thank you.'

Before she died, she seemed to feel better. She called me to her side and softly said to me, 'Giorgio, we were born at the same time, and have lived together twenty-four years, almost without ever being apart, and you've always been so very good to me. God bless you. But if I've ever upset you, or been rude to you, if I've not always shown the great love I have for you, forgive me.' Two tears slowly fell from her eyes. 'I'm sorry to die, I'm sorry for your sake. Your health is poor. You have need of a lot of loving care and' – after a long pause – 'guidance.' With these words she died. I sat up all night, alone, in her room, while old Maria sobbed and prayed in the room next door.

Her black eyes were open. Her black hair framed her white face; in marked contrast to that lugubrious whiteness and that funereal blackness was the pinkness of her lips, slightly parted to show the poor dead girl's teeth, which were even whiter than her brow.

A jolt to my leg roused me from my gloomy thoughts. I had a fever and my head was inflamed. I pressed the rigid blade of a fruit-knife to my forehead, which was burning hot. The coolness of it felt good.

The girl reeked of the sour stench of wine. I lent over to look at her: she was loathsome. She was sleeping with her mouth open. I then felt a sense of utter humiliation, acute remorse, and a kind of spirit of vendetta, at the same time raging and wary, stirred within my breast. I looked at the knife held was in my hand, balancing it to find the point at which it would deliver its most telling blow. Then, with one finger I delicately raised the girl's upper lip and gave a sharp tap with the tip of the blade to one of those pretty front teeth. The tooth broke, and more than half of it fell out.

The drunken hussy hardly stirred. I shoved some cushions under her head and went to open the window. Freezing fog entered the room like dense smoke. There was nothing to be seen, not even the streetlights. But from the entrance to the inn came the sound of trunks being loaded onto the omnibus. I was seized with an urgent desire to leave. The servant I called told me that this omnibus was just about to depart for the station, to catch the train to

Turin, but there was no time to lose. I put a 500-lire note into a sealed envelope, which I handed the servant, saying, 'Give this letter to the lady when she wakes, and send her home in a carriage. Then pack my bags with all that you find on the tables and in the drawers. Here are the keys. Send everything to my address in Turin. But first post me the bill, which I haven't time to wait for now.'

I threw my coat over my shoulders and left.

(Signor Giorgio's manuscript ends here)

These papers were entrusted to me by Signor Giorgio three days after he arrived back in Turin. He had returned from Milan all but cured of his serious stomach ailment, and more active, more lively than before. I felt relieved. He wrote for a good part of the day, and when I asked him, 'What is it that you're writing so furiously, Signor Giorgio?', he replied, 'I'm writing my ugly confessions and doing my penance.' Then he added in a most sad and resigned tone of voice, 'My dear Maria, it's a terrible penance!'

On the morning of the fourth day he was unable to get out of bed. He had a burning fever. After a long visit the doctor shook his head and as he left he said in my ear, 'This is the end.'

Signor Giorgio could no longer swallow anything, not even diluted milk. And his fever continued more violently than ever. He was so weak, he could hardly lift his arm. He raved almost the whole time. He talked to himself under his breath. I often heard the names of Giorgetta and Signora Emilia, and at such moments his face would take on a blissful expression of bliss that reduced me to tears. Then his face would darken again, and he would close his eyes, as though some fearful image was tormenting him.

One evening, the seventh after Signor Giorgio's return, a servant came to fetch me. My patient seemed to be asleep, and I dared to leave him alone just for a moment. There was a woman wanting to speak to him. She insisted, she shouted. What a woman! How vulgar she looked! How brazen in her speech and manners! Never had such a woman set foot in this house before. She claimed that Signor Giorgio owed her money, how much I don't know, and that she had come from Milan specially to collect it. I tried to quieten her, and just so that she would go I promised to let her in the following morning. She seemed prepared to leave, but as I returned to the bedroom, she quietly followed behind me, and Signor Giorgio, who had woken up, saw her. I put my hands together and begged her not to move and not to speak.

In the pale glow of the night-lamp, my poor sick Giorgio stared at that despicable woman. His face grew serene, and he beckoned her close with his hand. 'Emilia!' he murmured. It was a sweet delirium, and certainly full of many fond images that could be seen on the dying man's face. He wanted to say something, but he kept repeating certain words in such a faint voice that even I could not understand him. At last I managed to grasp that he was asking for the pearl necklace – a magnificent thing, his last present to Emilia, given to her a few days before she died. I took it from the cabinet and handed it to him.

He accepted it with both hands. And making an effort I would not have thought him capable of, and indicating to that dreadful woman to bend down, he very slowly placed it round her neck. He smiled with sublime tranquillity.

Having avidly examined the precious necklace, the woman twisted her lips in a smile of such base joy that it was a horror to see. A black gap, right in the middle of those white teeth, made her look even more sinister. Signor Giorgio stared at her, screamed with fright, then turned away, burying his face in the bolster, and breathed his last.

VADE RETRO,
SATANA

I

The priest stood motionless as he stared out, with his elbows resting on the windowsill. It was the first time in ten years that from his presbytery, in the highest village in the Trentino, he had seen a snowstorm down below, while the sun – a pale, almost frightened sun – shone on the houses in the hamlet and on the surrounding mountain-peaks.

Now and again the priest coughed. His bare neck was thin and white, and at that moment his lean, handsome face looked impassive. Yet anyone who had studied his features closely could have discerned the man within: he had two straight lines running from his nostrils to the corners of his pale lips; across his broad, open forehead was a deep furrow at odds with the gentle, almost childlike expression in his eyes, of an ultramarine blue, like the waters of Lake Garda. The artery in his neck pulsed strongly. His delicate hands were feverishly clenched. His fair hair, swept back by the wind, covered his tonsure. And meanwhile the stormclouds gathered, billowing like waves in some fantastic squall; like an inland sea, filling the whole wide valley, which crashed against the ring of mountains, as though trying to bring down rocks, woods, and glaciers, to engulf them all in its own depths that were darker than a tomb. Now and then, these depths came into view in places, depending on the eddying of the storm, when a gap opened in the surge of clouds. Then the eye penetrated down into the valley, where lightning flashed, whilst from above the banks of dense white cloud-vapour the flashes seemed no more than flickers. One of these dark holes revealed the village of Cogo. Then this chasm closed and another opened in the distance, momentarily revealing the tower of the castle at Sanna.

And the priest watched, sighing, with his fists clenched all the while. He had left his breviary open on the sill, and the wind playfully rifled its pages. But old Menico, who for some time had been standing behind the curate, muttering, seized the book with a typically petulant gesture, closed it and placed it on the writing-table. Then, gathering up the papers the wind had scattered on the floor, he said out loud, 'What's the point of trying to catch a cold! With nothing on your head and no scarf round your neck.' And slightly under his breath he added, 'You're crazy, completely crazy.'

He left the room, slamming the door behind him; but a moment later he was back, and went and fetched his master's skull-cap that was lying on the bed, and, standing on tiptoe, placed it over the cleric's tonsure.

The priest turned round in irritation and, seizing the cap, threw it to the ground in front of Menico, shouting, 'I'm hot, leave me alone.' Then he went back to watching the clouds, but within two minutes he turned round again, his eyes searching for Menico. He had gone. The priest went into the kitchen; no sign of him there. He went up to the next floor, a kind of attic half open to the rain and snow; Menico was not there either. He found him at the foot of the creaking, narrow, wooden staircase, an outside staircase, leading from the first floor of the building down to the churchyard, where five or six peasants discussing the novelty of the thunderstorm, continued to stare, wide-eyed, into the valley, where the thunder had stopped rolling and the lightning had ceased to flash and the clouds were clearing.

The priest went up to the old man and, holding out his hand, he said to him so that the peasants could hear, 'Menico, I'm sorry.'

The old man averted his face, shrugging his shoulders and keeping his hands in his pockets. He was small, thin and gaunt; his beard, shaved the week before, and bristling like pins, was not so much grey as white, but the thick eyebrows over his tiny little eyes were still inky-black.

The priest inclined his thin body and in a quiet, gentle

voice humbly repeated, 'Menico, please forgive me.'

The peasants sniggered.

All of a sudden the old man seized the priest's hand, not giving him time to withdraw it, and kissed it several times. And those tiny little eyes were shining with tears.

Back in his room, the priest picked up his breviary again. Having read scarcely two pages, following the text intently with his eyes and voicing every syllable under his breath, as the Church requires, he dejectedly closed the book. 'I can't,' he murmured, 'I can't. The office should be recited with attention and devotion: *Officium recitandum est attente et devote* ... Yet I feel in every limb a restlessness that I cannot explain, as though thousands of ants were crawling all over my body. I try to fix my mind on one thought or another, and my mind wanders where it will, delighting in a hundred strange and childish new images. It's probably the atmosphere, so charged with electricity today. Perhaps my usual touch of feverishness is getting worse.'

He went down on his knees before a gaunt crucifix, and remained there for several minutes, with his hands joined together, his head bowed, whispering prayers. Then abruptly standing up, he said, '*Oratio sine attentione interna non est oratio.*'

At that moment the priest's dog, a splendid hunting-dog, came bursting into the room, and began to bound around his beloved master, who patted him distractedly, and repeated to himself, while continuing to strike his aching breast with clenched fist, 'A priest should always be serene, like the sun just a little while ago; he should contemplate the storm from above, calm, pure, and intangible.'

The local doctor, who looked after the three villages in the Val Castra, entered without knocking. He was clean-shaven and smartly dressed.

'Good morning, Father. Hurry up and take off that jacket, put on your collar and your best coat, and come with me. The devil summons you, Father – but what a charming devil! She was frantic, and what she said was

117

this: "My dear Doctor" (she actually said that – "my dear Doctor"), "run over to the priest's house at once. Tell him how unwell I am, and say that I need to hear the voice of heaven, that I'm a lost sheep ready to return to the fold." And she kept saying, "I want the priest, I want Don Giuseppe.'"

The priest turned pale and solemn. 'Is she in danger of dying?' he asked.

The doctor burst out laughing. 'You want to bury us all, Father. It's an attack of nerves: a lady of leisure's ailment. I wasn't even allowed to take her pulse. She sent me over without giving me time to draw breath. And, I'll have you know, I've come straight from Ledizzo, on a donkey, with these stormclouds and lightning overhead. It's lucky I had my umbrella and overcoat. Well, Don Giuseppe, are you coming or not?'

'I'm not coming,' replied the priest, whose brow and throat had turned fiery red. And raising his fists, he added, in a voice fit to make the walls tremble, 'That woman and her protectors are an abomination, and they'll be the ultimate ruin of this valley, God damn them!'

The doctor was shocked, and looking the priest in the eye, he murmured, 'Father, some Christian charity!'

'Christian charity? I live on polenta and cheese, and a little pork occasionally, although my weak, emaciated body – which, as you know, doctor, is being consumed by a lingering but unsparing disease – ought to be better nourished. I live in the midst of this village's squalor, sharing the misfortunes of these mountainfolk, to whom I have given the little left to me by my father and what little I have earned in the last ten years. In the evenings during the eight months of winter I take it upon myself to teach the youngsters in the village, and there's not a boy or girl over the age of seven who doesn't know how to read and write and to distinguish between good and evil. I told the bishop, who wanted to send me to a parish down on the plain, "Monsignor, I now love the loneliness and the snow, the hardships and the ingratitude."

'I really do love the grandeur of this wild landscape, where my body has remained pure and where I have lived until now in a precious state of spiritual poverty. A little while ago I had to forsake my keenest worldly pleasure – hunting – and give up my long solitary walks along the mountain-ridges. My skin, once so rough and brown' – and the priest pitifully examined his own hands – 'has become soft and white, like a leisured lady's. They say that I look younger now that I'm so thin and pale. I'm thirty, and I pass for twenty. I'm turning into a boy again. Who's giving me back my health and strength?'

The doctor smiled, and the priest went on.

'One day in Trento the Vicar-General said to me ironically, 'You, Father, live in the mountains of Arcadia.' All but a few of my parishioners look at me askance. Christian charity!

'And then this village, the highest and poorest in the Trentino, where the men are hard-working, sober and honest, and the women have no other beauty but their virtue, is descended upon by a gang of swindlers and whores. They invent some story about mines. They proclaim from the rooftops that Nature has deposited riches of iron in our soil. The Tyrolese and German newspapers are full of advertisements and praise for the famous Valle di Castra Iron Company. Five thousand shares at five hundred lire each, with interest and dividends of at least one hundred per cent! They'll find fools to buy them, they'll pocket millions of lire, a considerable amount at least, and then clear out, leaving another two caves in our mountains – two empty holes. But meanwhile the head of the enterprise and his mistress take up residence here for a few weeks in a makeshift mansion, and there are servants, workmen and whores filling the village with scandal; taverns open, there's dancing all night long, and drunkenness, and worse. At the mines, at the ironworks, they regard us as simpletons. Three families from the village have already sold their heifers in exchange for these wonderful mining-shares: others will follow their example. The material ruin can be remedied, but there'll be no cure for the moral degradation. Two of the most innocent village-girls, one of eighteen, the other sixteen-year-old Giulia . . . '

The priest's thick, impassioned voice all of a sudden broke off after what had been a torrent of words. It had seemed that he would never stop; he had not even once coughed. Indignation had been simmering in that artless soul for some time, and now it had boiled over. But after what he had just said, Don Giuseppe became suddenly embarrassed and subdued. He studied the doctor's face for any sign that he had been able to guess what was coming next. And he was a little comforted to see that the doctor had his head bowed, as though stunned by the passion of his long sermon. The priest's eyes travelled to a corner of the room, and settled for a moment on the crucifix, which seemed to him even more blood-stained and sorrowful than usual, and he said a short but most fervent inward prayer. A deaf person, skilled at lip-reading, would have identified from the nervous movements of the priest's lips, a few fragmentary phrases: *Strictissima obligatio . . . inviolabiliter . . . sigillum confessionis.*

Meanwhile, the doctor was smiling, thinking of the priest's lack of sophistication. He himself had completed his medical studies in no less a place than Vienna, and during those eight months he had seen some really pretty girls. He had even told his wife about them, in scarcely veiled terms. Yes, gentlemen, in order to broaden the mind and not allow oneself to be ensnared by foolish and sentimental ideas; to acquire experience of the world, and to learn good manners, it is necessary to live at least for a while in the capital. Only bears can be reared in the mountains. The furthest the priest had ever been, poor fellow, was to Trento!

'Don Giuseppe, allow me to speak plainly: forgive me for saying so, but you seem to me somewhat pessimistic.'

Having spoken these words to test the ground, as it were, the doctor paused, awaiting a response. The response did not come: Don Giuseppe had assumed a composed and tranquil expression.

Plucking up courage, the doctor went on. 'It may well be, I don't deny it, that your expectations are well founded, and that some terrible catastrophe looms over this poor valley. But it could also turn out – who knows? – that things go smoothly. They're working in the mines, they've taken samples – it's not impossible that metal will be extracted, especially as there are vestiges of many old ironworks in our mountains. If the company were to do well, think of the wealth it would bring to all the places around here! Besides, once our noble banker has got his business going and his fancy for mountain life is satisfied, he'll depart with his entourage, leaving behind the real workers, the honest toilers. And everything will return to normal, with a bit more money and a few more amenities, which are certainly needed.'

'God willing!'

It was a 'God willing' interjected at that point just to change the subject. Indeed, without pausing, the priest went on to ask the doctor, 'Tell me, now, how's Signora Carlina today?'

'Not too bad, thank you. She's not eating much, almost nothing at all, although I make her come with me for the walk as much as possible.'

'And in good spirits?'

'So so. When I go out in the morning or after dinner on my medical rounds – what you might call my daily travels – she puts her arms around me and starts to cry. Sometimes, I confess, I rather lose patience.'

'Bear with her, Doctor. She's a child, and she loves you so much. I'll go further and say: try to treat her with infinite indulgence, with every loving care and kindness. Treat her like a tender and delicate young sapling, transplanted only three months ago and in need of being watered – with affection.'

'She's not really ill. A few headaches, that's all. But she's not putting on any weight. And then she's so unsophisticated: she would like to be on her own all the time, or with me. She hates meeting new people. In fact, to tell you

121

the truth, Don Giuseppe, I'm embarrassed. The lovely Baroness is desperately keen to meet my wife. As soon as I enter the room, she cries, "And where's the young bride?"

'For the love of the Virgin Mary, don't take her there. Don't let that disreputable woman's breath defile the honesty and modesty of that simple-hearted, eighteen-year-old girl, that innocent young lamb!'

'That's all very well, Father, but I'm dependent on everybody. I was born in this valley, I've no intention of dying here. To earn my living, every day I have to do three or four hours' walking along mountain paths, at the risk of falling down a precipice, freezing to death in the snow in winter, or dying young of heart failure. I save on a mule or a donkey, forcing myself − and being a bit of tyrant with my wife on this issue − to put aside some money that will allow me to move to a city, where I'll be able to practise as a real doctor. Letting blood, pulling out teeth, setting bones for these peasants is no decent profession for someone who has studied in the capital and has developed noble aspirations.'

'Nobility of aspiration, Doctor, lies in the will to do good. And it is all the more difficult to do good, but all the more worthy, the lowlier the object − and, I would add, the more unattractive − to which it is directed.'

'You're talking about perfection, Father. I admire sublime virtue, but not even according to the Gospel is everyone bound to be a saint. In the city, too, people may lead the lives of good men, and help their neighbour, and I feel I was born to lead a civilized life. Now, you see, Don Giuseppe, this lady − whether we call her a baroness, or whatever − pays me four florins a visit, and she summons me nearly every day. My piggy-bank thrives on it.'

'Signora Carlina would not approve of these sentiments, Doctor.'

'And wrongly so. Can I refuse the benefit of my knowledge to anyone who calls upon my services? There are no other doctors in the valley. It would take seven or eight hours to get one, and meanwhile, the patient is likely to die like a dog. Anyway, is it right to distinguish between a peasant and a lady, between an honest woman and a whore, or should not all be helped equally? Tell me, Don Giuseppe, if a sinner, man or woman, even without feeling at death's door, were to beseech a word of a minister of God, a word that might comfort, or improve, or illuminate an erring soul, would you have the right to deny it? To reach out to brethren who have sinned or strayed, to help them return to the straight and narrow – is that not the good pastor's primary and most sacred duty?'

These last words were spoken most emphatically by the doctor, who kept his shrewd eyes fixed on the priest's candid gaze. A silence followed, in which the villagers gathered in the square with the fountain could be heard singing and laughing. The priest was pensive. With a movement of decisiveness, he went and fetched his clerical collar from the wardrobe, fastened it on without looking in the mirror that hung from a nail in the windowframe, and which he used to shave his beard, and put on his black jacket, the only one he possessed. Then he said, 'Let's go.'

At that moment a great din of trumpets, horns, cornets and other brass instruments that screeched and squealed abominably joined the peasants' ever-mounting hubbub; and in response came the sound of firecrackers let off outside the village, on the mountain-ridge. It was a special holiday: the orchestra from the neighbouring town, no less, had been brought in; and the ceremony was presided over by the Mayor. What was actually taking place was a real triumphal march. The heroes were two twelve-year-old boys, one dark-haired, the other fair; they were crowned with wild flowers, and were riding in one of those vehicles used in the mountains to transport manure – with their curved fronts, these look somewhat like ancient Roman chariots. The cart, all festooned and garlanded, was drawn by two stately white oxen, but instead of a conqueror's boldness, the two boys displayed a great fear of being hurled to the ground as the wheels either climbed over the enormous rocks with which the steep, narrow, winding paths of the village were strewn, or sank into swampy holes from which mud splattered out. The two young lads gazed round, bewildered by so much noise and anxious for only one thing: to jump down from the triumphal wagon in order to join their companions and be free to run around, shouting, 'Hurrah! Hurrah!'

The reason for their great glory was explained by Menico to an old pedlar selling those enormous red and blue umbrellas that, when it rains, add a touch of brightness to the gloomy landscape. What had happened was this: at the beginning of the previous spring, the two boys went up Mount Malga – the one that casts the longest shadow in the Castra Valley – to collect the roots of a certain medicinal plant. This is one of the ways that mountain-folk make a little money: at the risk of falling down chasms and breaking their necks, they earn a few pence for a considerable weight of arnica, gentian, monkshood, lichen, or goodness knows what else, gathered from the rocks on the craggy peaks. The snow was melting at the bottom of the mountain, but, scraping it away as they went, the two boys singlemindedly climbed higher and higher to a place that had not seen a living soul for eight months. Suddenly, they heard a rustling from under a pine tree that the wind had blown down – with its trunk and dry branches lying on that blanket of whiteness, it looked like a skeleton. They listened. There was more rustling. They went nearer, and out came a brown animal, like a small dog. The animal fled and took refuge in a thicket; the boys went after it. They had two sticks and began to beat at the thicket – which, although leafless, was dense – one on either side, with all the strength they could muster. They wanted to catch the dog. And indeed, the animal, frightened and provoked, came out, but instead of running away, it rushed at the arms of one of the boys, bit him, and drew blood, which made the snow turn red. But, nothing daunted, the more the boy felt himself being bitten, the more he stood his ground. And along came the other with his stick and landed a timely, heavy blow on the animal's

124

head, then a second blow, which killed it. More cheerful than ever, the injured boy held his arms in the snow for a while, then he and his companion went leaping down the mountainside, carrying their prey.

They were not sure whether it was a dog or a wolf. But before they reached the village, they met a tall, wiry old man of eighty, whose body was still as straight as a ramrod, and as agile as a roebuck; he was out walking with his rifle slung across his shoulders. The fame of this old man has travelled beyond the Castra Valley: even in Trento they know of him. He has killed twenty bears in his time. The last, after his gun misfired, he killed by grappling with it: the man plunged his knife into the bear's belly, and they rolled some way down the mountainside, still locked together, until the bear died. Then this octogenarian calmly got straight to his feet.

Now this old man called out to the boys as they went past, and said, 'Where did you get hold of that creature, boys?'

The boys replied, 'We killed it ourselves. But is it a wolf or a dog?'

'It's a bear-cub, you lucky young fellows − lucky that you didn't find its mother, and lucky that you've earned yourselves a handsome thirty-seven silver florins. Go and claim them from the Captain.'

With that, he continued on his way, looking up at the glaciers on the mountaintops.

Menico pointed with his umbrella to one of the high-landers in the crowd who towered almost a whole head over everyone else, and who was gazing seriously at the two little heroes: it was the old bear-hunter.

To cut a long story short, a few months later the boys had been able to collect the thirty-seven florins that the Governor gives as a reward for any bear killed; and the festivities were to commemorate and celebrate the event. In the interests of truth, it has to be said that some devious minds had seen it as another excuse to spend the whole night dancing with the band at the inn, squandering the money on debauchery and excess. And because the priest well knew this, he had not wanted to involve his church, or himself, in such riotous goings-on. And besides, his own bear-hunting caused the priest no little remorse. He, too, had come upon an unweaned bear-cub one winter in the snow. He had caught the cub and hit it a bit, making it yelp, so that the she-bear, which could not be far away, would hear it. And sure enough, she came rushing up in fury, while the priest took careful aim and found his mark. Mortally wounded, the she-bear dragged herself over to her young, which continued to yelp, and licked it in a gesture of infinite love. The priest went home wrapt in thought, leaving the dead mother-bear in the wood and letting the cub go free. That evening he searched through the books in his small library to find out whether there was any harm in deceiving when used against wild beasts, but he failed to find anything relevant to his case. The only thing he found, in the second volume of Gury's *Compendium theologiae moralis*, was that a priest is permitted to hunt in a seemly manner, *cum sclopeto et uno cane*. That was all. But he could never forget the selfless and deep passion of that dying mother-bear, and whenever he thought of it he felt a pang in his heart.

He said again to the doctor, 'Let's go.' And they went out, leaving behind the noise of the village festivities.

II

The banker-Baron's villa was an improvised creation. At a short distance from the village stood a house made of stone and cement – an extraordinary phenomenon in that entirely wood-constructed village. It had been built ten years earlier by an honest soul who, having spent half a century working down in Italy as a boiler-maker and accumulated many thousands of lire, wanted to enjoy them with his family, in blessed peace, amid the clean air and deep snows of his beloved birthplace. If only the idea had never occurred to him! The day the first stone was laid, his daughter suddenly died; the upper floor had no sooner been laid than his son killed himself falling down a cliff; hardly was the roof finished when his wife passed on to a better life. The poor fellow – alone, inconsolable, and full of aches and fears – spent a year pacing the empty rooms, recalling with unutterable longing his days of poverty, when his wife and children, all healthy and strong, ate nothing but polenta and he spent fifteen hours a day hammering at boilers and frying-pans. He died at the age of seventy. leaving his house to the Commune, which used it for storing hay, since no one would pay any money to go and live there – partly because everyone was accustomed to living in rickety wooden shacks, partly because of the idea that the building was jinxed and brought misfortune.

There was no glass in the windows any more, the shutters were beginning to fall off, but the big house – so white and tall and well proportioned, with its fine terrace and overhanging balconies – was a joy to behold amid the dark huts and hovels in the surrounding landscape. Furthermore, it stood in the loveliest spot: on the spur of the mountain, from which all the villages in the entire valley could be seen dotted here and there, with the eye travelling to the green plain beyond, and the castle at Sanna. And behind, it was shaded by a dense copse of age-old larches, whilst in front lay a bright meadow, on almost level ground, full of big elder shrubs with their red berries that looked like blazing coral, and densely carpeted with pink flowers swaying on very tall stems, and yellow, purple and white flowers that would make the prettiest and most colourful coronet for a bride.

The boiler-maker's already attractive house had become enchanting. At the front, on the ground floor, was a new loggia, with drapes that seemed to be made of wonderful Persian cloth, drawn during the hours of sunshine; extending on either side were two new pavilion-shaped wings, with four steps descending to the meadow that had been transformed into a garden, complete with symmetrical flowerbeds, a large round pond of clear water with gold-fish, and swings scattered in the most secret and shady places. Behind the building was a new portico where horses could shelter while waiting for their riders; the kitchen, stables, servants' quarters and other places that served a menial purpose were located in a kind of rustic cabin linked to the big house by a covered walkway, which was all hidden by climbing vegetation and trans-planted shrubs.

These additions to the building were made of wood, hastily erected, and intended to last three months: it did not matter that the next snowfall and frost would destroy them all.

The person who had supervised all this work was the actual discoverer – or, to be more accurate, inventor – of the mines, a notorious scoundrel compared with whom the president of the mining company, the banker-Baron, could claim to be a saint. He was called Gregorio Viorz, and it was rumoured that he had twice been to prison for fraud. He was also said to be guilty of a poisoning, carried out for personal gain, but the evidence was lacking and the authorities had never stepped in. Be that as it may, after all the things he had done in his native town of Innsbruck, he could never set foot there again.

Unluckily for mankind, God had endowed him with the most fertile ingenuity and matchless energy, so much so that with half the effort and thought he expended going about his dark and devious ways he could have made himself rich and respected and certain of his own success. But the inevitable corollary of a wicked nature are certain fatal weaknesses that spoil everything, and Viorz had two such weaknesses. Firstly: he was too sharp, so that having worked out all the dangers of any undertaking, and doing his best to anticipate them all, he often created difficulties in the very process of trying to avoid them. Secondly: as the time to reap the fruit of his misdeeds gradually approached, the joy and arrogance of his success went to his head, robbing him of his composure, and in tackling the final obstacles his initial wily caution turned to brutal violence.

A person of this sort could not lend his name to any industrial or banking enterprise, so he had to remain shrouded, at least initially, in prudent mystery. Therefore, he needed someone to act as a front man: not a gentleman, for none would have had anything to do with such crookedness; nor a notorious scoundrel, for instead of attracting people he would have scared them off. What was needed was, for instance, a fellow who had consumed his inheritance; a degenerate in urgent need of funds; sufficiently intelligent to understand the ins and outs of the business and to go along with it, but not very inspired, so that he did not one day take it into his head to act on his own initiative. A fellow with nice well-bred manners, a good family name and an impressive-sounding title. And in addition to all these qualities, he needed one other: that of being totally unknown to men of the banking class, or better still, of being someone of whom they had a favourable knowledge. This requirement, along with the all the others, was met by Baron von Steinach.

He was an irresponsible man of no convictions rather than a truly wicked person. Moving in elevated circles in Vienna and Paris had inured him to every vice, without resulting in the loss of his charming aristocratic manners and a certain sensitivity of nature. He had been involved on three or four occasions in some big and much talked-about crashes, but he had unconcernedly and unfailingly met his losses, repaying every last penny. After he met Gregorio Viorz – who never subsequently lost track of him, and who called the Baron in great haste a few years later, as soon as the idea of the Mining Company first occurred to him – Steinach went to Monaco, borrowing the money to gamble, and won. And with these winnings he settled in Paris, and began living the life of a captain of industry. One way or another, he survived, always dressed in the latest fashion, although with a touch of Teutonic gaucheness, living in small but splendid apartments, full of artistic baubles, reigned over by one or other of the women – blonde, brunette, tawny or red-haired – that he picked up here or there, and replaced every six months at the outside. And so he reached the age of sixty, still robust and full of life, which seemed a miracle, considering his dissolute-ness and debauchery. Nor did his age reveal itself except in two things: the roundness of his paunch, which in his customary white waistcoat looked even more imposing, and in his continuing to live, for more than a year now, with the latest Baroness, a red-head, without feeling any desire whatsoever to replace her with another.

The priest had not said a word during the walk from his house to the villa, despite all the doctor's goading. His mind seemed elsewhere; he watched the freakish clouds covering part of the sky with their whiteness.

A servant in turquoise livery with crimson braiding and big gold buttons showed the two visitors into the room where the Baron and the rest of the house-party were relaxing after a meal, and asked them to wait there until the Baroness might receive them. The Baron, who was sunk deep in an armchair, smoking a cigar, rose, went over to the priest and, shaking him by the hand, said lots of agreeable things to him. He had been anxious to meet him. He knew of all his virtues, and he wished to help the poor of the parish. He knew that the Baroness had been to deliver alms to the presbytery when she first came to stay in the villa; however, he himself wanted to do something longer-lasting. He had in mind a hundred charitable schemes, but to put them into effect he was awaiting the advice of a wise and saintly man to guide him, and teach him to do good usefully.

This courteous behaviour, this open smile, above all these generous offers placed the poor priest in a terrible quandary, confronting him again with the same old di-lemma: can I reject the devil's money? Can I deprive the poor of the help they so badly need? Should I not rather solicit this largesse, whatever its provenance might be, leaving God to enter the hearts of sinners?

The Baron continued to stand there talking, in front of a window overlooking the entire valley, at the far end of which could be seen the bright, winding river, like a ribbon of pure silver fluttering in the sun. Meanwhile, in the opposite corner of the room, the Baron's guests chatted round a circular table covered with books and magazines. All of a sudden, the Baroness's piano instructor, a short young man with a pair of spectacles perched on his nose, who had been a not very successful student at the Dresden Conservatory, removed the wrapper from one of the illustrated magazines, and read the first page, exclaiming, 'Oh wonderful, magnificent, truly marvellous.'

Then having shown the engraving to the rest of the group, who echoed each other's admiring oohs and aahs, he bounded up to the Baron to show him a view of his villa, no less. There was the verandah with its draperies; there were the pavilions with the four steps, but with the addition of two domes, each with a Fortune on top, as envisaged by the architect who had done the restoration. And there were the fountains, with new water jets – in short, a palace. Beneath was the caption: 'Home of the President of the Castra Valley Mining Company.'

As he glanced at the engraving, the Baron murmured to himself, 'How cunning of that fox Viorz!' And he returned the magazine to the music teacher, who began to read out the accompanying explanatory article. It was a hymn to the new company: its metal-rich mines and Vulcanian ironworks. Already the workforce was insufficient to the task, and commercial demand outstripped the company's production twenty times over. New breaches needed to be made in the sides of the miraculous mountain, and the number of mines increased, with new shares to be issued by the bank. Then came the artistic and sentimental parts: descriptions of the villa and garden; and the President hailed as a benefactor, a real godsend, a true Messiah to the valley, responsible for the founding of nursery schools already attended by three hundred children, who were given free breakfast and lunch as well as instruction; for the new roads under construction, and the pharmacies now open, et cetera, et cetera – a veritable regeneration.

The piano master read bombastically, emphasizing the finest phrases. He ignored the Baron, who, breaking off his discussion with the priest, called out, 'Enough, enough, you can read it later.' But the priest was no longer paying attention to his interlocutor's flattery; instead he was trying to listen to the reading, edging closer and closer to the round table. At a certain point, without waiting until the end, he snatched the page from the reader's hands and tore it into shreds, saying over and over again, 'It's all lies, all lies.'

The Baron left the room; the doctor vanished. There was half a minute's silence when no one moved. Then an officer of the Alpine corps, who was sitting next to the piano teacher, rose to his feet. He went up to the priest, and after a tremendous bellow of anger, he shouted, 'Count yourself lucky – if it were not for your calling and your clerical collar . . . ' And he raised his arm menacingly.

At that moment the servant in the turquoise livery with crimson trim and big gold buttons entered and announced from the doorway, 'The Baroness is ready to receive the Reverend Father.'

The priest inclined his head in parting, and slowly left the room.

III

The servant opened the door to the Baroness's room, gave a deep bow, then withdrew, leaving the priest alone with the woman. In the first instant he did not see her, for the room seemed wonderfully ablaze, dazzling the eyes. The wall-hangings, sofas, and armchairs were all of red fabric, a vivid rose-red, patterned with sinuous yellow designs, like flames. And the setting sun – warm, bright and golden – shone through the two wide-open windows, casting upon the red and yellow of the room a kind of incandescent glow and brilliance that looked like fire and sparks. A penetrating, heady smell of perfume emanated from a dressing-table that was all frills and lace, standing beneath a canopy held aloft by a winged putto, while in front of the mirror-frame, decorated with glass flowers, sparkled countless little flasks of white metal, and combs, and soap-dishes, and clear crystal phials, and every kind of knick-knack.

The priest felt a rush of blood to his head as he came in; he had a desire to run away. The woman called to him in a soft voice, like a distant lute.

She was reclining on a sofa in the only shadowy corner of the room, along the wall in which the windows were set, right back where the folds of the full curtains cut out the light to the side of them, leaving a kind of recess between the drapes and the wall.

'Sit here, beside me, Father, in this armchair. I feel so weak, I can only just talk in a very low voice.'

The priest replied curtly, 'Forgive me, I'm in a hurry. I only came because the doctor told me you were ill and needed me. What can I do for you?'

'Oh, I'm so ill! But that unfeeling doctor doesn't understand at all. A good and learned man like you, Father, is capable of finding the words to comfort and hearten me, and by restoring my faith in myself and the world, perhaps restoring my physical health. My illness lies here.' She touched her breast.

She wore a floral-patterned robe revealing all of her neck, a good deal of her white bosom, and the tops of her round shoulders, over which fell her loosened, wavy hair, of a reddish-blonde colour, that grew low on her forehead in unruly little curls. She had a nose that met her forehead in an almost continuous line, with a strong, wide bridge, and flared nostrils through which she occasionally snorted like an Arab horse. Full lips, round cheeks, and a receding chin gave a kind of sheep-like and lascivious expression to her face. The redness of her mouth was a little too intense, the pinkness of her cheeks a little too delicately shaded, and the shape of her brown eyebrows a little too finely arched to be able to believe that art had nothing to do with it. And she had a slight shadowing beneath her blue eyes that made them look bigger. In short, she was in her own way beautiful, and sensual.

The priest remained standing. Exerting herself, she rose, went over to him, took him by the hand and, leading him two steps forward, made him sit in the armchair. Then she fixed him with her eyes, and stretched, as though she had just wakened, so that her wide sleeves fell back, baring her arms almost to the armpits; and her bosom swelled proudly. She turned and threw herself onto the sofa, letting her embroidered slipper fall from her right foot on to the floor. Those blue eyes were now smouldering.

Her voice no longer sounded soft and weary as before. A dry, choked, irritable tone was predominant when she said to the priest, speaking in fitful bursts, 'Tell me, Don Giuseppe, why do you avoid me? Why do you not want to see me any more? When I ride through the village on my mule, why do you close the shutters of your house in my face? And why, having received me in the presbytery four times in the beginning, have you now given orders not to let me in, not even when I bring money for the poor? I can't set foot in the sacristy, and I'm all but chased out of the church like a dog. The gifts I make to the church are returned to me. By what right? Who can possibly refuse offerings made to God?' She leapt to her feet and planted herself in front of the priest, with the question, 'Is it that hate is a Christian virtue, Father?'

The priest said in a voice that was calm but trembling, 'Hatred of evil is a Christian virtue.'

'Christian virtue, Father, is love. I was taught so as a little girl, when I went to catechism in church. I was told the same thing in the confessional. Then, when I became a woman, I saw that true love raised my spirit, purified my soul, brought me close to heaven. True love came to an end, through no fault of mine, I swear. Poor and forsaken, cast into a society full of temptation and corruption, I was taken in by what seemed like love. But seeming-love is not

134

love, it is hate; it is in fact the vilest, most ignoble, most fearful, most harrowing hatred possible to experience. This hatred is killing me. Yet I have a passionate heart, which for many years has sought in vain the solace of a fierce and genuine affection. I need ardent love.'

Making a supreme effort to gather his thoughts, which kept slipping from his mind, the priest murmured, 'Peace, my poor child, calm your imagination, which the misfortunes and setbacks in your life have over-excited. Strive to desire one thing: that which is good. Quit the life you are leading, this mire of false illusions and depravity that is sullying your existence. Go back to being poor and lonely, but repentant and righteous. Then everyone is bound to love you, for, in loving you, they will love virtue.'

'And you, Don Giuseppe, will you love me, too?'

And she took his hand and pressed it, while the priest drew closer.

The woman went on meekly, 'Don Giuseppe, guide me. Teach me the way, lead me wherever you will. I shall be your slave. I shall, if you like, be your saint. You must surely have a great and noble heart that mirrors the sky, as your eyes do. I like you because you're pure and handsome, because I suspect you have never loved, and because I want to be your first sin, your first remorse. Give me your love, Don Giuseppe, give me your love.'

The Baroness sank back on the sofa, still holding with both hands the hand of the priest, who was trembling from head to foot. The sun had set; the room was growing dark. But as the woman repeated these last words, all at once the priest seemed to feel a fresh breeze upon his forehead. And suddenly there appeared before him the sad and bleeding figure of the Christ over his prayer-stool, except that the face, instead of being bowed and dead, was alive and staring at him with an extremely fierce and forbidding expression. The priest sprang up, and before the woman could utter a syllable, he had left the room.

When the servant dressed in turquoise livery with crimson trim saw the priest hurrying away from the villa,

135

almost running, without a backward glance, as if he had the devil at his shoulders, he smiled maliciously, placing the index finger of his right hand on the tip of his nose.

IV

Unconscious of what he was doing, the priest turned left, where the road goes up into the mountains. He passed below the chapel of San Rocco, set on the summit of a sharp crag, and headed towards the so-called Lake Meadow. He passed some of those alpine carts that have front wheels only, and two extremely long shafts whose rear ends trail along the ground, which are used to carry bulky loads of freshly cut grass, fragrant with every sweet smell and spangled with little flowers of every bright colour. Obedient to the commands of the mountain-folk leading them, the poor oxen, majestic and resigned, slowly and solemnly descended the steep slope, firmly planting their hoofs amid the huge boulders, their liquid eyes looking a little worried and rather melancholy. The women greeted him, but the priest did not respond. Once he was almost run over by a cart he had not made way for in time. He left the road, and made his way along the paths, up the bare rocks. The night had grown dark, and the priest pressed on without knowing where he was treading. Suddenly he found himself on the edge of the mountain lake fed by glaciers, where at last was brought back to his senses by the sound of the two mountain streams that came rushing down from the peaks and crashing through the rocks; by the harsh wind blowing through neck of the valley; and by the hacking cough that racked his chest. And falling on to his knees, with his hands joined together and his eyes fixed on the utter blackness of the heavenly vault, he made a long prayer of thanks to the son of God.

Menico, meanwhile, was getting increasingly worried. The presbytery clock had struck half past midnight and the priest was still not back. The old man had seen the lights in the baron's villa go out, and he knew very well there were no one dying in the parish. So where on earth had that reckless fellow gone to spend the night? He dared not go too far from the house; he looked through the windows, but saw nothing but pitch darkness. Had he not been a priest's servant he would certainly have allowed himself some gross blasphemy. He strained his ears, for a dog had barked, but no one came. He heard a distant sound of tramping feet, and listened again, but no one came.

'Oh, Father is going to have some explaining to do, staying out all night without even giving me any warning! Is that a way to treat people? And at the risk, what's more, of catching some new illness through such unholy behaviour, and with that blasted cough he can never get rid of. Really, is this a time to be wandering the streets and keeping decent folk out of their beds? I intend to give him some plain speaking, some really plain speaking. He would try the patience of San Luigi Gonzaga.'

He stared out into the darkness again, listening. There was no sign of anybody. At last he thought he heard a man's tread some way up the road. It was definitely a man, coming down the mountain. The footsteps quickened, resounding loudly; the dogs barked; it was the priest. Then the little old man went and stood at the door with a sullen look on his face, his eyes flashing with anger. He had his hands on his hips in an attitude of defiance, as though he wanted to deny the priest entry into the presbytery, and his lips were already parted to begin his tirade when he saw the priest's face, and kept silent, letting him pass.

He muttered between his teeth (or, to be more precise, between his gums), 'My goodness, what a high and mighty expression! And what a state his clothes are in! It'll take me a month to mend them and get them tidied up again. That's fine Christian charity for you!'

The priest spent the rest of the night on his knees, before the crucifix, which had saved him. Dawn made the Christ on the Cross, with his bowed head crowned with thorns, look yet more livid, emaciated, contorted and bloody.

At daybreak the bells began to chime. It was Menico who rang them, getting a young boy to help him when he was busy in the church and sacristy, or when his arms felt tired – usually one of the lads whose triumph had been celebrated the previous day; in fact the dark-haired one, who had not seen a penny of his half-share of the thirty-seven florins' reward for killing the bear-cub, so swift had his family been to eat and drink it all away.

It was Sunday, and the priest's mass was supposed to start at ten. At about eight a peasant, who came from the valley, handed Menico a letter for his master. The address, in a neat, flowing, elegant script, appeared to have been written by a woman's hand. The priest took the letter and stared at it. His fingers burned, his hands trembled. A dreadfully alluring vision of a half-naked woman passed through his mind, and he thought he heard in his ear the seductive and frightful echo of a voice that whispered, 'Give me your love, Don Giuseppe, give me your love!' The priest desperately wanted at all costs to know who had sent the letter, but the peasant was surely well on his way by now, and Menico had not noticed which direction he had taken.

'Anyway,' remarked the old man, shrugging his shoulders, 'open it and you'll see who's written it.'

The priest went ahead and tore open the envelope, unfolding the sheets of paper, of which there were several, with an attitude of dread. But he quickly brightened, and sat down to read the letter. It was from Signora Carlina, the doctor's wife:

'Dear Father,
I have need of all your patience and indulgence. Good, kind Don Giuseppe, you've been so sweet to me in recent months that I have no hesitation in opening my heart to you completely, in all its sadness, doubts and fears. When I feel that I am not behaving as I should, you chide or comfort me, but above all you give me guidance, for my experience being so limited and I of such a timid disposition,

unfortunately, that not only can I not make up my mind to act, but often I don't really know which path to choose. Bear with me, Father.

I'm eighteen: I ought to be almost a matron by now, yet until only three months ago, until my wedding-day, I had lived like a child, with my father, a good but most austere man, and my mother, the devoted housewife. We never saw anybody. I had no enthusiasm for reading. I embroidered. I liked cookery books, indeed I willingly spent time in the kitchen, bringing, I confess, to the art of cooking, especially sweet dishes (you must come and try one, Don Giuseppe, the first day you have time – arrange it with Amilcare), bringing to it, as I say, a touch of ambition. Besides, I was said to be of delicate health. You, Father, sometimes stare into my face with a look full of compassion, as though to say, "The poor girl is so thin and pale!" Amilcare has, as he puts it, "listened" to me several times, and found not the least trace, he says, of any illness. The fact is that I never have to stay in bed, and I can seriously claim to be a great walker, a real alpinist. And that reminds me, I would like you to persuade Amilcare not to make me walk so much. When he goes into the mountains visiting his patients, he almost always wants me to go with him. Yesterday, when it was so sunny, at about two in the afternoon, he took me along the mule-track shortcuts as far as Masine: an hour and a half's climb, and such a rocky climb! When we reached the village I made straight for a seat in a corner of the church, a damp and cheerless church where I had to wait a good two hours before Amilcare had finished doling out remedies and drawing blood, and meanwhile I felt quite numbed by the freezing-cold air. I haven't the courage to say no. Amilcare quite rightly says that walking stimulates the appetite, and that I need building up and ought to eat more, especially meat, and to drink at least one glass of wine. But I really dislike wine, it's no affectation to say so, and tiredness robs me of even the little desire to eat that I would have had.

Father, you know the circumstances of my marriage.

Amilcare is my only cousin. I can honestly say that he was the only young man who ever came to visit our house during the autumn months. He's kind, and handsome, and well-mannered, with his own lively way of talking. He studied hard, and in Vienna he distinguished himself. He graduated and became the local medical officer in this valley. To cut a long story short, what daydreams I used to have! I would stay awake at night so as to be able to pursue my reveries, for it seemed to me that the whole day was not long enough for such infinitely precious thoughts. My father did not seem very happy. He was not very pleased that I was to marry a doctor. He said that all doctors are materialists, a word I did not really understand, but did not like at all. And he made out that living in this valley was as good as being buried: with eight months of winter, six feet of snow, the temperature thirteen degrees below freezing, no woman could leave the house, and she would have all the worry about her husband – the problems were endless. And inwardly I thought the opposite: for me, winter would be paradise: with two nice warm rooms, flowers by the stoves, my embroidery, my little kitchen, a few letters to Mama, and first and foremost, my ever-kind, ever-charming, ever-cheerful Amilcare! What long talks we would have, and how happy he would be to come home to his little house, and to his Carluccia, who would love him so much! Forgive me, Father, I'm such a silly goose. So we were married. The honeymoon was heavenly, and the first month in this valley delightful. To tell the truth, however, even from the start Amilcare used to smoke a little too much, fouling the air in the bedroom. I didn't say anything, but sometimes I found it hard to breathe, and felt slightly queasy. But it was nothing serious. My husband loved me. He was always talking about the future, when we would move to a city, and his name would become famous, and he would earn so much money, and be showered with honours, and throw big parties, where I was to be dressed like a real queen. I wasn't very happy about this last bit: I've never had much inclination for social gatherings. Certain little things already made me apprehensive, upset me slightly; he was at fault.

The problem began quite suddenly, when that woman they call the Baroness came to live in the villa next to you, Father. On the first day of her arrival she sent someone rushing over to fetch my husband. Since that moment he hasn't been himself. He is full of grand schemes. He seems to be ashamed of me, and yet he makes me follow him on his walks in the mountains, but he doesn't look at me, or speak to me; he doesn't even help me when it is steep, or to cross a stream. And at home, if I speak to him, he answers yes or no, or doesn't reply at all. When he does eventually speak, it is only to criticize, or, what's even more hurtful, to make some sarcastic comment: that I don't know how to dress any more, or do my hair; or even put a spoon in my mouth, or use a knife and fork. He finds the house small. Neither lunch nor dinner is to his liking, no matter how much effort I put into trying to guess what will please him, and into preparing and cooking his food. He's dined four times at the tavern with the carters, and even on other evenings, when he's not at the villa and not visiting his patients, he goes and drinks gentian liqueur there, and (I'm ashamed to say) has more than one glass, for certain. And then afterwards! Father, good, kind Don Giuseppe, help me. I'm at my wits' end, and don't know what to do. I can't say anything to my father or mother. You, Don Giuseppe, are the only person on earth who could understand and help me.

And I'm becoming wicked, too. I do my best to be loving and sweet to him; he rejects me, and I become meeker than ever. But sometimes I can't. I feel, rising within me, a violent sense of rebellion that is utterly new and incomprehensible to me – which, after all, runs completely counter to my natural compliance. I'm experiencing something I've never known before: deep acrimony and bitterness. Now I know the taste of gall. I understand so many things I knew nothing about before: an ugly world is opening up to me. I examined myself in the mirror. Yes,

141

I'm thin. Yes, I'm pale. But I can see that my eyes are big and black, my forehead, mouth, and features are all regular, and my body's by no means a skeleton. Yet my husband of only three months no longer finds me attractive.

He talks of the Baroness's rounded charms. I've seen those brazen charms: on three occasions she passed beneath my windows on her white mule, followed by her servants and admirers. I stared at her and took a good look at her face: she wears rouge on her cheeks, colouring on her lips, and her magnificent eyebrows are pencilled. She's as outwardly false as she must be inwardly deceitful. And she has robbed me of Amilcare's respect and love. Now, one last word, Father. Amilcare wants me to go and visit his beloved. I've said no. He insists, but I won't, come what may. Am I right or wrong?

Don Giuseppe, lend me a guiding hand. You who see the things of this world from the lofty heights of your blessed tranquillity, tell me how to escape the baseness and depravity of these new fears, suspicions and anxieties of mine. How I have changed within a month!

Most unhappily yours,
Carlina'

The priest had read the letter closely, sighing at first, trembling by the end. 'Poor sainted woman!' he exclaimed. And in his large and hurried handwriting he wrote the following note: 'I'll come tomorrow. We'll talk, and you'll see that your suspicions are groundless. Patience, kindness and love – these are the remedies. Pray to the Most Blessed Virgin Mary, who knows the weaknesses of mortals, and their distress. Until we meet tomorrow.'

Menico had announced a little while ago that a woman, Pina del Rosso, and her aged father wanted to speak to the priest. They came in now, their eyes filled with tears, and the woman sobbed as she told how her husband wanted to sell their heifers, all twenty of them, their sole asset, in order to invest the money in the ironworks company. 'He's supposed to take the animals to market in Malè the day after tomorrow, and there are five or six others possessed by demons who are also taking their herds. They'll be giving the beasts away for nothing. And anyway, I don't believe in such companies – may the devil take them. They're nothing but a swindle. My father says so, too, and he knows the way of the world.'

And the poor half-paralysed old man concurred with a mournful nod of his head.

'I should never have said so to my husband! He lost his temper, and beat me. Look at these marks.' And she showed her bruised shoulders. 'But I kept on at him, and he went wild. I couldn't dissuade him at all. You save us, Father. Write to Trento, write to the Emperor. For pity's sake, don't let the village be destroyed.'

The priest had risen and was pacing up and down the room in the greatest agitation, as he listened to the woman. He kept saying, 'Villains.' Then he said out loud, 'I shall speak to the Mayor, I shall confer with him, and with God's help we shall succeed in doing something.'

'The Mayor! A fine help he'll be!' said the woman. 'He's the one who's been putting ideas into people's heads. He's the one who suggested to everyone they trade their animals, which give them so many problems, he says, and so little profit, in exchange for those sheets of paper that you only have to look at and they produce solid gold. I heard him with my own ears, Father. Our poor herd! And then (dare I mention it?) to anyone who said that Don Giuseppe didn't believe in such miracles, the Mayor replied, 'Ah yes! That ... (I won't say the word out of respect), that ... we'll drive him out of the village, and the sooner the better. It's time we got rid of that ... He can't see further than the end of his nose, and he presumes to tell people what's what.' Then under his breath he added, 'It won't be long now, you know, a week at most, I have it on good authority, and that'll be the end of him.'

The priest continued to pace up and down, filled with rage. 'Well, then, tomorrow I'll go to the Captain of the Militia in Malè, I'll appeal to the magistrate, I'll bring proceedings against those scoundrels.'

From the threshold of the room, Menico said, 'Father,

it's almost ten o'clock, come and get robed for mass.' He had to go up to his master and repeat this several times, for the priest was so beside himself.

Don Giuseppe tried to regain a little of his composure. He said goodbye to the woman and the old villager, left the presbytery, crossed the churchyard, and entered the vestry through the outside door just as the young wolf-killer was ringing the final summons to worship.

While Menico bustled about helping his master put on his vestments, the priest pounded his breast, over his heart, as though trying to stop it beating, and whispered prayers.

He walked to the altar with his eyes on the ground, without seeing anybody. He bowed before the steps, then went and kissed the holy table. And as he uttered the ritual words he inwardly made these devotions: 'I am unworthy to approach the altar that holds the relics of the saints; I am unworthy to be admitted to the divine table at which the Holy of Holies offers himself as the Eucharist. O Lord, let me not give you a kiss like the one Judas gave you. O Lord, save me from such wickedness by cleansing my spirit ... *Oramus te Domine* ... *Kyrie eleison* ... O merciful Lord, you have given men so many blessings, and how they have repaid you with evil. Behold before you the most ungrateful, the most guilty of all. Forgive me, Lord. Forgive my weakness, have pity on me ... *Gloria in excelsis Deo* ... '

Still with his eyes to the ground, the priest turned to face the people. And while his lips read the Epistle from the right of the altar, he silently murmured, 'Lamb without sin, who was willing to be vilified, mocked and insulted, in order to fulfil the prophesies in the Scriptures, let me imitate your innocence in my deeds, and your patience in my afflictions.

He turned to the left and began the reading from the Bible: *Munda cor meum* ... Word of God, who in your graciousness show meekness and humility, let not meekness and humility ever forsake my heart ... *Credo in unum Deum* ... '

The priest removed the lid from the chalice, replaced it again, washed his hands at the side of the altar, turned to face the congregation, and still with his gaze lowered, he said, '*Orate fratres.*' Then he held up the host, in memory of Christ raised on the Cross, and having consecrated the wine, lifted up the chalice.

'O precious blood, let this new baptism flow over me. If only I could shed all my blood for you, to the very last drop . . . *Per omnia secula* . . . '

The priest broke the sacred host in two, as a symbolic reminder of the separation between the body and spirit of Christ, and dropped a piece of the host into the chalice. He then swallowed the wafer, striking his breast. '*Domine non sum dignus* . . . ' Afterwards he drank the precious blood from the chalice. And having taken communion, he proceeded to the ablutions. '*Dominus vobiscum* . . . In the ineffable joy of seeing you rise up into heaven, O Saviour of the world, I feel the happiness of still possessing you here on earth. My faith adores you on the throne of your love in the Eucharist, in the same way that it adores you on the throne of your glory in Paradise . . . '

With the words '*Ita missa est*', the priest looked up and saw Olimpia, the Baroness, seated at the head of the congregation, in the front pew, next to her piano master. Her snow-white neck and the top of her milky bosom gleamed in the semi-darkness of the church. Her full, red lips smiled, as she met Don Giuseppe's gaze with brazen lustfulness. The priest felt a veil come down over his eyes. He could not see. He staggered. All his blood ran to his heart. A moment later it all ran to his head, and then he could not control himself any longer. Adopting the same attitude as Christ in Michelangelo's 'Last Judgement', in a thundering voice he launched into a wrathful sermon from the very steps of the altar.

'Stay away from the house of the Lord, sinners and hypocrites! Be gone, profaners of the temple. I would seize Christ's scourge to drive away these corruptors of souls, these deceivers of consciences, these greedy parasites that feed on the money of the poor. And you, misguided souls, blinded as you are, do you not see what precipice opens beneath your feet? You're ruining the village, casting into destitution your children, wives and old folk by chasing after illusions. Open your eyes, my sons. Believe me. With all my heart I've been father and brother to you for ten years. I would rather die a hundred deaths sooner than leave this beloved mountain. Believe me. And I beseech you, as I prayed moments ago to God, lord of all things: acknowledge your error, return to your simple, honest ways, to the care of your beasts, to the love of Him who truly loves you. You shall have peace on earth and joy in heaven. Remember God's commandments. Regarding the sixth, canon law condemns the woman who beautifies herself to please men. As for the seventh and ninth, it condemns those who steal by violence, fraud, or false promises. Be gone, sinners. May God help and enlighten you.

V

Having given vent to his feelings, the priest returned to his room. White-faced apart from two pink circles in the middle of his cheeks, his throat dry, his breast inwardly consumed with flames, he was coughing, and spitting large spots of blood into his handkerchief, but felt quite calm, while outside, by contrast, the storm gathered against him. In church, at the sound of his terrible voice thundering beneath the vaults, no one had dared to breathe. But afterwards, once the sermon was over, on the way out, almost everyone was whispering, and questioning each other, and exclaiming in scandalized tones. Anyone who had not quite grasped the meaning of the words had a companion explain them. The Baroness had vanished. The Mayor had rushed off to order his mule to be saddled, intending to ride over to Trento in order, he said, to get this raving lunatic finally sent to the asylum.

The next day, no sooner was it light than the priest, despite his fever, walked down into the valley. Then from Cogo, where he got a ride on a peasant's cart, he went to Malè to see the Captain of the Militia, who listened with some impatience to what the priest had to say, and told him that his own information was different: there was no danger, and no reason to get so worked up. In any case, these were matters for the civil authorities, not the Church, so he should calm down and go home.

On his return, disheartened and exhausted, the priest stopped by to see Signora Carlina, who was on her own. He remembered the letter he had received the previous day, and he set about trying to comfort her with judicious arguments. But as he spoke, tears ran down his cheeks, and his breathing was laboured. The good-hearted young woman graciously silenced him, and kindly made him take a little broth, half a glass of wine and two slices of a cake that she had made with her own fair hands. The priest calmed down, and listened to that soft, gentle voice, as the poor girl, forgetting her own distress, tended to her dear Don Giuseppe. She did not want him to leave, and with her hands joined in entreaty she begged him not to continue on his way. But the priest kept saying with a sigh, 'I shall do my duty.'

When he left the house, he felt stronger, lighter and purer. Before starting off up the mountainside, he retraced his steps some twenty yards, to kneel at a roadside shrine. A light shone on the Virgin's image, which was certainly not one painted by Fra Angelico or Raphael. Set around her reddish-yellow hair, which was drawn in wavy lines down to her shoulders, were the rays of a large halo, like the spokes of a wheel. She had pink cheeks, while her crudely shaped mouth was a bright scarlet. And so neat and precise were her semicircular eyebrows, they must have been drawn with a set of compasses, centred on her blue eyes. But when, in the fervour of his prayer, the priest looked up at this image, he thought it must be some trick of the Devil. It looked to him like a ghastly caricature of

Olimpia, and he suddenly felt his heart pounding horribly, and he frantically got to his feet.

Thoughts seethed in his brain, but a trifling one kept coming to the fore, and it was this: 'Are that disreputable woman's lips, cheeks and eyebrows painted, or not? Was Signora Carlina right about what she had seen, or had a blameless jealousy clouded her judgement? And at the idea that she might have been deluded, the priest had a sense of vague regret. Then, feeling ashamed of such unseemly thoughts, he tried to pick up the thread of his interrupted prayers, but the more he concentrated his efforts upon banishing the lewd woman's image, the more stubbornly this vital, imperious, seductive and supremely beautiful image confronted him.

Already at five in the morning, the following day, the priest was sitting in the confessional-box, hearing and pardoning the village women's humdrum sins. It was St Roch's feast-day, and before bringing their candles to join in the procession from the village church to the saint's shrine that was to take place at about four in the afternoon, these pious women wanted to set their consciences at rest. With every absolution the priest repeated to himself, contritely and devoutly, the verses of the fiftieth psalm, and in order to overcome his tiredness and boredom he went over in his memory the good confessor's guiding principles, especially those given by St Alfonsus Liguori, whose teaching was always to observe the golden mean, inclining *neque ad destram rigorismi, neque ad sinistram laxitatis.*

Some twenty penitents had already received the *Ego te absolvo* when the priest smelt a most delicate fragrance, like that of violets, and through the small holes in the close-meshed grille saw a very dark shadow. In the enclosed gloom of the confessional, it was impossible to distinguish the features of the person's face, which were covered, moreover, with a black, embroidered veil.

The priest began in a tone full of benevolence, 'Let us thank the Lord, my child, who has today brought you to confession. Don't be afraid. I'm really the vicar of his love, *vicarius amoris Christi*. God wants to comfort you, so take heart. I shall help you. Whatever may have befallen you, with divine help we shall put everything right. Speak then in holy confidence.'

'Father, it is I.'

The priest leapt up and was about to leave the confessional-box. But then, thinking this might be a temptation of the Devil, he clutched the crucifix that hung from his neck and murmured a prayer.

'Father, it is I,' repeated the dark shadow's voice, 'and I want you to listen to me.'

The priest sat down again, thinking that it was not right to refuse a penitent, and with big beads of sweat dripping from his brow he stammered, 'Have you repented? Truly repented? Do you know what contrition means? It means abhorrence of any sin committed, and a firm resolve to mend one's ways.'

'Don Giuseppe, I've come to save you.'

'Does this concern only myself?'

'Only yourself.'

'Then this is not the place. Write to me.'

'I can't. What I have to say to you must remain secret.'

'Under the seal of the confessional?'

'Under the seal of the confessional.'

'Then I warn you that you must not name any guilty parties or accomplices: the Synods have formally ruled against such denouncements.'

'I'll tell you what they're going to do. I'll reveal no names. Don Giuseppe, you're an obstacle. They want you out of the way.'

'I shall fight.'

'Don Giuseppe, they want to kill you.'

'I'll look after myself.'

'They're going to poison you tomorrow. Beware of the wine cruet. Lock up the sacristy. Change the wine. Smash the cruet. Save yourself. Goodbye.' And the dark shadow disappeared from the church, while the sun was beginning to gild the top of the belltower.

The priest resumed his confessions with the same patience and gentleness as before. He was busy all day with the procession, with visiting priests from the valley to whom he had to offer some of the wine that he had – a very light, slightly acidic wine – and with many other duties and obligations. He made arrangements for the following morning's ceremony, when St Roch's statue, which had been solemnly brought from the shrine to the village church, had to be taken back. And having said good-night to Menico, he finally retired to his bedroom, more dead than alive, although his temperature had dropped and his cough had given him some respite.

Immediately after Olimpia's disclosure, the priest was like a new man. His uncertainties and worries, and self-dissatisfaction; the ignoble wrestling with his own imagination; the relentless battle against his own senses; the fear that he had already fallen and committed some mortal sin, through his weaknesses – all these things had bowed him down physically and prostrated him mentally. Now he had suddenly straightened up and taken heart; he had suddenly assumed an air of gladness, almost of boldness.

'I shall die,' he kept repeating, 'I shall die on the altar. I shall quit this vile cloak of flesh. I shall become pure spirit. There'll be no more conflict, no more remorse, but eternal peace.'

Yet during the day he began to suffer some scruples. Could he drink the wine regardless? Was he not obliged to submit himself to these earthly woes for love of his neighbour? Was the secrecy of the confessional to override the priest's own safety, when saving himself could not possibly give rise to suspicion against anyone? He searched through the Synod's rulings and the *Roman Ritual*; he checked in the *Tractatus de Sacramento Poenitentiae*; he consulted the writings of Cardinal de Lugo, and Coninck's *Confessione*; he examined the works of St Thomas. Nowhere were any exceptions allowed to the inviolability of confessional secrecy. In fact, to his utmost consolation, the priest came upon a case identical to his own, that of Blessed Father del

Bufalo; having been told that the eucharist wine was poisoned, the founder of the Missionaries of the Precious Blood went ahead just the same and celebrated mass, using the wine from the cruet, and died. In short, whatever the cost, the priest always had to ignore what he heard in the confessional, even at his own expense. Having unequivocally resolved this fundamental issue, Don Giuseppe gave effusive and most warm-hearted thanks to Christ, at his prayer-stool, before retiring to bed and falling into a long and peaceful sleep after such turmoil.

Menico had to shake his frail body several times before the priest managed to wake up properly.

'Much good may it do you, Father!' said the cantankerous old man. 'It's time to get up. Can't you hear the bells ringing for mass?'

'I'm coming, my good Menico, I'm coming.'

And within twenty minutes he was already robed in the sacristy, and blissfully reciting the *Veni Creator*. He entered the church as though entering Paradise. His eyes were joyful. He had never walked so majestically. It was as if he were climbing the steps of God's throne in radiant joy. '*Introibo ad altare . . . Introibo ad altare . . .*' But there was no sign of Menico, who was supposed to be doing the responses. At last he emerged from the little doorway of the sacristy, carrying the two glass vessels on the small tray, and he came hurrying up to the altar. But a figure dressed in black, with a veil over her face, rose as he came past her, and in an apparent rush to leave the church she collided with the little old man, causing the tray and cruets to fall to the ground. There was a great crash, and the vessels broke into a hundred pieces. The water and wine formed two little puddles.

It is impossible to describe the ensuing commotion. Who could it have been? Was it . . . ? A woman. She was gone. Had she done it deliberately? And that fool Menico! Now what would happen? Mass could not be celebrated any more. The church would have to be reconsecrated. It was a warning from heaven.

'Go and fetch the cruets from St Roch's shrine.'

This advice was immediately followed, and a quarter of an hour later the service could resume. After mass came the procession, with the appropriate banners, and the children dressed as angels, as usual, amd the customary green and red cloaks, and the usual grumbling. The painted wooden statue of St Roch, with his broad-brimmed hat, pilgrim's shells, and his hand pointing to the sores on his leg, was returned to its niche in the shrine, and the ceremony came to an end. The priest desperately needed to be alone.

When he entered the presbytery he saw two people standing by the window in the hall, who must have been waiting for him. They were the Mayor and a clergyman, who had just arrived from Trento. He invited them to sit down, but with a grieved and humble demeanour the clergyman handed the parish priest a large letter stamped with the Bishop's seal. The priest read the first lines, and turned pale. He asked if he might withdraw to his room for a moment. He leaned back against the wall and continued to read, then fell to his knees before the bleeding Christ, and prayed for a few minutes.

The letter suspended the priest from his parish duties, and ordered him to hand over the church, together with all its sacred objects, and the presbytery, with everything that was not his personal property, to the clergyman who brought the letter – and did so (should he think of applying to the civil authorities) by agreement with the Mayor. As for the reasons for such a severe sentence, the letter had little to say. It cited this maxim: 'Parochus debet, in quantum potest, cum debita prudentia scandala de medio tollere.' Now, not only had the priest lacked prudence in seeking to root out scandal, he had given rise to further scandal of the most serious nature, refusing to cease his questionable – or, to say the least, his rash and morally imprudent – behaviour. Having lost all authority in the parish, he was to surrender his office to others. Signed: Giovanni, Bishop of Trento.

The order was final. He had to obey. He called Menico, asking him to parcel up his small amount of linen, his cassock, a pair of shoes, three or four theological tomes – nothing else. He put in his pocket the daguerrotype portraits of his late mother and father, and went out into the hall, saying, 'I'm ready. Let's begin in the sacristy, if you like.'

The clergyman was not expecting anything to happen so fast; Don Giuseppe should take his time; there was no hurry; in fact, he wanted to say how dismayed he was; he wished it to be known that he would not have accepted but for his oath of obedience. Don Giuseppe insisted, and they began to make an inventory of each and every object. This task should not have taken long, the church being so poor and the cupboard in the sacristy so small, but the new curate wanted to examine everything closely, and he remarked in an unctuous voice, in honied tones, 'O God, how dirty! Blessed Virgin Mary, how tatty! There's a piece missing! There's an oil stain on it! How beggarly! What a disgrace!'

There was a moment when Don Giuseppe faced the suave cleric and, impatience making his speech rapid and broken, he said, 'Father, the parish is extremely poor! I've given the church all of the little that I had, right down to the very last coin. I did the best I could. Forgive me.'

The other became even more saccharine and obdurate. He named the objects in Latin and meticulously examined them one by one. '*Purificatorium lineum* . . . it's all ragged! *Mappa triplex ex lino vel cannabe confecta* . . . there are two holes in it – no, three, four! *Calix et patena* . . . made of brass, and how dented they are! *Missale cum pulvillo* . . . there's not a page without a corner missing! *Paramenta albi, rubri, viridis, violacei et nigri coloris* . . . oh, what faded colours, you can't tell one from another any more! *Bursa, velum, manutergium* . . . these aren't worth keeping! *Ampullae vitreae* . . . There were no cruets. And at this point the new curate's face took an expression that was a mixture of outrage, disgust and pity, with his head tilted to the left and his hands joined in front of his mouth.

In the presbytery Don Giuseppe said, 'I'm leaving behind everything except, with your permission, this bundle.' And he showed them what was inside. He went on quickly, as if the words burnt his lips, 'Mr Mayor, please accept this hunting rifle in memory of me. I ask you, Father, at your discretion to distribute a little money to the poor of the parish, in payment for this furniture, all these things here – which are my property that I'm leaving behind.'

Having carefully examined every corner of the room, the clergyman nodded his head, solemn and aloof.

Don Giuseppe went on in a weak voice, choked with sorrow: 'Then, if you would do me a favour, Father: convey a last farewell to my . . . forgive me, to your good parishioners, from a poor pastor without a flock. I've loved them so much, and must leave them, after ten years, without saying goodbye, without a single word of affection. It breaks my heart to go away, and I have only a few days left to live, but in those few days I shall pray for them as a father prays for his beloved children.' Tears welled up in the poor man's eyes.

From the road leading straight out of the village, the priest quickly set off downhill, accompanied by Menico, but after a hundred yards or so he stopped, as though he had forgotten something of vital importance. He stood there for a moment, thinking. Then steeling himself, he went back and knocked at the door of the presbytery.

When the new curate saw him standing before him again, he could not repress a gesture of annoyance. And an embarrassed, timorous Don Giuseppe whispered, 'Forgive me, Father. A minute only: have pity on a poor priest whom you will never see again. Be generous – please, don't be angry. There's a gift I would ask of you, the greatest gift I could possibly receive in this world.'

Impatience, scorn and avarice showed in the other man's eyes, but he had that perpetual smile on his lips.

Still standing at the door, Don Giuseppe went on timidly, humbly, as though begging for charity, 'In the bedroom there's a Christ on the Cross. It's my only comfort, and I've always prayed to it, and it has always helped me and saved me from the temptations of the flesh. Without that Christ, I could not live or die in peace. Father, have pity on me, give me that Christ.'

The new curate went over to the prayer-stool and examined the wooden figure. It was crudely carved and ineptly painted, with red drops of blood spurting from the brow crowned with thorns, and gushing from the gaping wound in its side. The body's limbs were all twisted, and the long, thin, white face inspired terror and disgust. The worthy cleric took the Christ down from the wall and handed it to Don Giuseppe, saying, 'I prefer a more kindly, attractive image of the Son of God. Religion needn't serve to terrorize children and the wicked. Gentle souls, like mine, yearn for gentleness. Take it, and God be with you.'

Menico was waiting outside the village, with the bundle in his hand. He wanted to carry the crucifix as well, but Don Giuseppe would not let him. he had wrapped it in a piece of green canvas, but he held it carefully under his arm, as though it were made of glass. It was actually made of such worm-eaten bits of wood, so badly stuck together, that had it fallen on the ground it would certainly not have remained in one piece.

Master and servant kept looking at each other, without uttering a syllable. It was getting dark and the road was deserted. The priest felt a weakness of the kind that follows high fevers, and his forehead was bathed in sweat. He sat down on a rock, practically on the ground, burying his face in the palms of his hands, with his elbows on his knees, and wept. Then looking up at Menico, he said, 'And I'm blameless, Menico. As far as I know, I've done nothing wrong. I resisted the Devil, I defeated him. I loved my parishioners.' And he covered his face with his hands again, weeping.

Menico plucked up courage and finally asked a question he had been wanting to ask for some time. 'Father, where do you intend to go?'

'To Cogo, this evening.'

'And after that?'

'I don't know.'

'So what next?'

'I put my trust in Providence.'

'Providence is all very well, but, forgive me, Father, have you any money in your pocket?'

'No.'

'Of course, you couldn't have any. You gave it all to me to do the shopping. But if I didn't remember . . . ' and he handed the priest an old purse, adding, 'Here's one hundred lire.'

'A hundred lire, how can that be? I can't possibly have given you that much.'

'You did, Father.'

'Tell the truth.'

'Well, there's some of my saving as well.'

'Your entire savings – tell the truth, now. And you're left with nothing.'

'My needs are few.'

'You've a heart of gold. But I don't want all this. I'll take twenty lire.'

'Sixty, at least.'

'No, twenty.'

'All right, here's twenty.' Menico was lying; he had left Don Giuseppe with sixty.

'Now, you go home, Menico, it's nearly dark. It looks as if there's a storm brewing. Give me the bundle and return to the village.'

The old fellow was not at all willing. He meant to go down at least as far as Cogo and spend the night there. The sky would have cleared by the following day. But in fact Menico was already dead tired; he was limping and tripping over every stone on the road, so he simply had to stop. Then the priest kissed the weeping old man on the fore-head, and said goodbye.

Not even the hunting dog that had come following after his master, leaping up around him, wanted to turn back.

And as he patted the dog, Don Giuseppe conscientiously considered whether he might now draw a little comfort from the faithful animal's lively affection, but feeling ashamed of his profane desire, he inwardly ruled against it and murmured, 'For me, the world should no longer offer any consolation.'

Having been tied to a string and led away by Menico, who walked at a snail's pace, the dog could only follow at the old man's heels, with its tail between its legs. Unsettled and its suspicions aroused, the beast gave long drawn-out, heartrending howls that carried through the mountain silence like voices of sad omen.

When the priest was unable to see him any more, Menico collapsed on to the grass, muttering, 'That's fooled him. He thinks I'm going back to the village. In fact I'm going to rest a while, then go down to Cogo to join him, and just let anyone try to keep me from him!' He kept repeating every now and then, 'What a business! What a terrible business!'

VI

The priest was left on his own.

There was a bend in the path just at that point, where it came winding into another narrow valley, from which the alpine village was no longer visible. Don Giuseppe turned round to gaze at his church, and his mountain, and to rest his eyes once more on the icy peaks, which stood out white against the clouds in the monotonous grey twilight. The poor man did not cough; he felt no fire in his chest; he did not have the feverishness and hectic flushes that he suffered almost continually. And he thanked heaven for granting him an hour's good health on the day when everything else that he owned on this earth had been taken from him. Only he felt a weariness in his every limb that was not without a certain pleasantness and lulled his mind into a state of vague and almost dreamy drunkenness.

As he passed through the village of Ledizzo, he looked up at the windows of the house where Signora Carlina lived. She was looking out into the street, waiting for the doctor, and saw her good, kind Don Giuseppe walking slowly in the last glimmerings of twilight. She greeted him and cheerfully invited him to come up. This lovely creature's pure voice seemed to the unhappy priest to come from the heavenly heights.

'It's the good angel,' he murmured, and quick as lightning this thought brought to mind the wicked angel, the Devil in its terrible beauty. Then, drawing back the green cloth from the bleeding face of the Christ held under his arm, he kissed the wooden statue as though imploring his own salvation.

But Signora Carlina insisted. 'Come up, Father, do. I've so many things to tell you.'

The priest did not reply, and continued on his way. But twenty yards on, as he came to the little chapel where he had stopped two days earlier, now feeling faint and dizzy, and his legs unable to support him, he went inside. In the dim, flickering light the crude image of the saint once again appeared to him to be the diabolical likeness of Olimpia.

Half an hour went by. Signora Carlina, who had seen the priest enter the chapel, from which a pale glow illuminated a brief stretch of the path, not seeing him come out, was troubled, and beginning to suspect that something was wrong she went down there with her maid to see for herself.

Don Giuseppe lay collapsed in a corner, giving no sign of life: with his arms hanging loosely and his head tilted back, with unseeing eyes and the slack mouth of a dead man. Help was summoned, and the poor priest's body was lifted up, gently carried to the doctor's house and laid on the bed in Signora Carlina's room. She had sent in great haste for her husband, wherever he might be at that time of day, at the Baroness's house or one of the drinking taverns. Holding her breath, with light fingers she loosened the priest's collar, unbuttoned his undershirt and placed her left hand on his naked chest. She thought she felt his heart beating. Then throwing herself down on her knees, she said several times over, 'My good, kind Don Giuseppe! Oh, God of mercy, spare my good, kind Don Giuseppe!'

Then she immediately began to feel again whether his heart really was beating.

The priest gave a sigh so light it would not have made a candle-flame flicker. But the young woman noticed it and a lovely smile of hope sprang to her lips. She lowered her cheek to the invalid's pale lips to check whether a little breath was actually escaping from them.

Indeed, he was breathing. He opened his eyes, looking dazed, but his limbs remained stiff. The first thing he asked for, which Signora Carlina understood more from the movement of his lips than from the sound of his words, was this: 'My Christ, my crucifix.'

It had actually been found, carefully laid on his bundle at the shrine, and been brought to the bedroom. Reaching up on tiptoe, Signora Carlina placed the foot of the cross on the chest of drawers and rested the Christ against the wall, right opposite the bed, so the priest could see it without moving his head. The cross stood out black against the pale brightness of the wall, set between two coloured lithographs in gold filigree frames, one of which showed Paul and Virginie at the ford, the other picturing the young girl's death and her despairing lover.

The bleeding, gimcrack Christ looked more terrible than ever there in that neat and pretty room, which was kept spotlessly clean, without a speck of dust: with flower-patterned curtains, freshly starched and laundered; white bed linen, with raised embroidery and lace trim, worked by the skilful fingers of the lady of the house; needle-point in woollen yarns of every colour on the armchairs and seats; and tassels and bows and braiding that she had made while innocently dreaming of a modest and virtuous paradise, into which had strayed a little while ago the vague wish that her Amilcare were like her good, kind Don Giuseppe.

Don Giuseppe was no longer staring at his Christ. He had a different expression on his face: he looked frightened by some vision and at the same time drawn to it. He gazed at the ceiling with his eyes wide open, as though to see better, and also he had his mouth open with his lips protruding, as though to draw in something. He was whispering in a feeble voice, now full of terror, now full of relief, '*Vade retro, satana.* Lucifer. Beautiful, fair-haired and wicked woman, your hand is a burning pincer. Cover your feet and your bosom. Quiet! Your love, Don Giuseppe, I want your love. I'm your slave. A kiss . . . Get behind me, Lucifer. No, come, temptress, come into the midst of the flames. Let me embrace you. Give me your lips, let me suck them, I want to see whether you have coloured them with rouge. Look at me with those blue eyes of yours, let me examine the shadows beneath them to see whether they are the work of a brush or of lasciviousness. Saint and whore, rays of gold shine from your hair, brighter and more glorious than any nimbus or halo. Cover your head, for pity's sake. I cannot look on your neck or breast: like the glaciers on the lofty peaks of my mountains in the light of the noon sun on a hot summer's day, your neck and bosom blind me. Ah, don't hold me so tightly in your soft, pink arms, you're hurting me. Yes, hold me tight, suffocate me, crush me, quickly – see the flames leaping about us, already burning our feet, legs, hearts, heads . . . '

Signora Carlina strained to hear. Her cheeks were pink with shame and her eyes full of tears. She kept saying, 'He, too! He, too!' And she covered her face with both hands. To put a stop to his ravings that were breaking her heart, she raised the priest's head, and cried, 'Look at your Christ, Don Giuseppe.'

The delirious man's gaze fell on the cross, which gradually had a calming influence on him. He quietened down. His lips began to whisper prayers, and his pale face cleared, becoming serene and gentle once more, regaining its innocent, almost ethereal expression. And Signora Carlina, reassured, exclaimed, 'How beautiful you look, my good, kind Don Giuseppe, now heaven is mirrored in your face.' And the priest began to breathe more freely, and already he was able to press in his own hand the hand of his artless nurse. Very slowly, she lowered her pure lips close to his pure brow. Don Giuseppe did not notice; smiling, he kept his eyes on his crucifix.

At that moment came a great crash at the front door, followed by the sound of an unsteady and heavy footfall making the wooden staircase creak, then the bedroom door flew back on its hinges as the drunken doctor burst into the room. The impact made the furniture shake. Then the Christ overbalanced and fell to the floor, shattering into countless pieces. The head rolled into a corner of the room, the arms, legs, and torso went scattering here and there, and red blood seemed to spurt from the dismembered limbs. The priest observed this destruction with staring eyes. Then, overcome with a mortal dread that contorted and disfigured him in a manner horrible to behold, he gave a shriek that ruptured his heart.

When the doctor, who reeked of brandy, reached his bedside, Don Giuseppe was dead.

THE GREY BLOTCH

This grey blotch clouding my vision may be the most common thing you know of as an ophthalmologist, but it bothers me greatly, and I would like to be cured of it. You can examine my cornea, pupils, retina etc. with your stylish equipment, when I arrive in two weeks' time. Meanwhile, since you ask as a friend, I shall describe my new ailment to you as best I can.

In bright light my eyesight is as keen as a lynx's. In the street during the day, at the theatre in the evening, I can see the beauty-patch on a woman's cheek at a hundred yards' distance. I can read a book printed in the tiniest English typeface for ten hours at a stretch without tiring. I have never needed glasses. Indeed, I can count myself amongst those 'animals of such superior vision' that, as Petrarch says, 'they can look into the sun'. I have never loved the sun so much as during the last two months: as soon as dawn breaks, I open wide the windows and bless it.

I hate the dark. In the evening, as the light fades, a formless, ash-grey blotch before me, just where I settle my gaze, gradually intensifies. At twilight or when the moon is shining, it is very faint, almost invisible; but in the darkness it shows up very strongly. Sometimes it is still, so that the night sky, when I look up, appears to have a light, ragged-edged hole in it, like one of those paper hoops used in the circus, after the clown's body has gone through it. And visible through the hole is what appears to be another, ugly sky beyond the stars.

Sometimes it moves, growing bigger and smaller, broader and longer, throwing out octopus-like tentacles, snail's horns, or frog's legs. It becomes monstrous. It circles round to the right, then to the left, spinning wildly before my eyes for hours at a time.

I use these images just to try to make myself understood, but it does not actually have any shape at all. In the month

165

that I've had to put up with this unsightliness, I've never been able to identify it as any particular shape. Whenever I think I see a likeness to some animal or object, however fantastic, to something definable at least, that shape instantly mutates, and becomes bafflingly contorted. It is a gross, obscene thing. If you could smell it, it would stink. It's like a big muddy stain, an animated blotch, a live, purulent sore. It's horrible.

I'm not saying that I see it all the time. I see it every night, but for longer or shorter periods of time, depending on my own disposition, whether physical or mental I do not know. Often, thank God, it no sooner comes than goes.

The terrible thing is that it looms up in front of me unexpectedly, when I'm thinking of something completely different. I was holding the hand of a lovely young girl by the dying light of an oil-lamp, telling her things not to be repeated even to you doctors, and then all of a sudden there was the blotch staining her breast. I was horrified.

And during the day, if I go into a dimly lit church, for instance, I risk coming upon this obscenity lurking under the dense shadow of the organ, on the old smoke-blackened paintings, or in the dark grille of the confessional-box. The fear of seeing it makes me detect it all the sooner.

At night I never look with impunity upon the waters of a river or the sea. I went to Genoa some days ago. It was a lovely evening, a last vestige of summer. The sky was utterly calm, of the same scarcely unvarying shade of colour from east to west, tinged with a little yellow, green, purple, and yet, almost on the horizon, was an isolated area of thick cloud. A very narrow, bright strip of air shone between the cloud and the sea. The sun, which had remained hidden by those clouds for a while, dropped below their lower edge and dipped into the tranquil waves. At first, when all that you could see of it was the lower segment, it looked like a golden lamp suspended from the clouds; then the fiery orb's circumference touched both clouds and sea for a minute, until it slowly sank into the water, its upper segment like the mouth of a huge oven revealing an incandescent blaze within.

I had dined very well with an old friend of mine. We took a boat and rowed out to sea. After the splendour of that sunset the twilight was of ineffable sweetness. We sang quietly, dreaming. Darkness fell. The dark green water glinted and glistened. Suddenly I saw my grey blotch floating a long way off in the distance. I fearfully withdrew my gaze to the confines of our boat, but my blotch pursued me among the oars and rowlocks. Chilled with horror, I had to endure its loathsome company all the way back to land.

(Don't laugh, doctor), my retina must be damaged: there's some kind of blind spot, a little area of paralysis, in other words, a scotoma.

I have read how, in the eyes of men condemned to death, the image of the objects on which' they last gazed has been found on their retinas, after the poor wretches' heads are cut off. So the image on the retina is not just a fleeting picture, but in some cases the image actually remains engraved upon it.

And bear in mind that when I close my eyes to sleep, I can feel my blotch inside me. And then it's a different kind of torture. The blotch is no longer fixed to the same spot in its permutations – it wanders, and goes rushing about. It shoots up and in doing so pulls my pupil up after it, so that it feels as if my eyeball must be revolving in its socket. Then it shoots down, then from side to side, and the eyeball follows it, almost tearing the ligaments, and after a while my eyes are aching, really and truly aching. In the morning and after I've had a nap, they are sore and slightly swollen.

You doctors have the virtue of being curious. You want to find out what causes things, to trace them back to their origin. So I shall tell you the circumstances in which the ailment that you must cure first manifested itself. And be patient, because I shall do so in the most undiscriminating detail, for I know how you scientists can glean from one of these trifles that escape the layman's attention the glimmer of understanding that sheds light on the most hidden truths.

On 24th October last, at nightfall, I was crossing the Ponte dei Re at Garbe to go to Vestone, on my usual after-dinner stroll (my morning walk used to take me to Vorbarno, when I did not prefer to go climbing up mountains, or to make a short excursion, also on foot, to Bagolino, Gardone, or the Tyrol). Of the two and a half months I spent in Val Sabbia, the first two weeks were all peace and quiet, the next two all excitement, and the remainder sadness and terror. In preference to the beauties of nature that everyone goes rushing to see, and everyone admires, I had opted for this poor modest valley, where the mountains have a certain wildness about them, and there is no danger of ever seeing the lean figure of an Englishman, or the black beard of an Italian mountaineer. I ate lovely pink trout from Lake Idro, tasty crayfish, mushrooms, wild birds, goat's cheese, and lots of eggs, and polenta.

There's a little inn at Idro with two small, clean, airy rooms. For anyone with a clear conscience, it's a blissfully peaceful life there – without newspapers, coffeeshops, or gossip – spent gazing at the lake, at the youngsters rowing, at the fort of Rocca d'Anfo on the far side; exercising the legs more than the brain, in fact gradually growing dull with the blessed, cherished freedom of having absolutely nothing to think about and nothing whatsoever to do.

When clouds are sent racing across the sky by the wind this landscape becomes infinitely changeable in appearance. The mountains that crowd around, the rocks on which stand the ruined walls of castles or chapels with their white belfries, and the low hills crowned with pine trees undergo a transformation every minute. Sometimes the clouds cast the foreground into shadow, and the sun shines in the distance; at other times the sun shines in the foreground and it remains dark behind; and there are yet other occasions when this part or that in the centre shows up dark in the midst of light, or light in the midst of darkness, and countless splashes of extremely bright, varied colours are constantly bursting into view and disappearing.

The thing to do is to climb the rocky mountain opposite the chapel of San Gottardo, on the other side of the Chiese. It's a vertical drop down the mountainside to the river. On that curious hill to the right stands the tall, thin church of Sabbio, and on the left, discernible in the distance, is the fort of Rocca di Nozza, of which only a few crumbling walls remain, while below, at your feet, yawns a deep abyss. You can hold on to the bushes with your hands and look down. The Chiese curves round, its swift-flowing waters breaking over the enormous rocks lying scattered on the riverbed. Low down, and a little to the right, is Garbe, and further away, much higher up on the mountain, is the bell-tower of Proviligio. Almost directly below, although on the opposite side of the very narrow valley, which becomes even narrower at this point, scarcely wide enough to hold the river and the postal road, is the chapel of San Gottardo, whose tower, seen from above, is so foreshortened that it looks dwarfish, and the arches of the small portico appear flattened.

The first time, I was all but overcome with dizziness. I tried to go up higher, where the almost sheer, bare rock offers virtually no footholds between its tight fissures. I looked round. The mountain behind me stood out as a shadowy mass against the blue sky.

It must have been about five in the evening, two weeks after my arrival in Garbe. The sun was beginning to sink behind the mountain. A fresh breeze was blowing through the neck of the valley and I had to hold on to my hat to keep it from falling into the precipice. But while I was using both hands to collect heaven knows what strange leaves, a sudden gust caught it in a spin, then sent it bouncing off, from one sharp, jutting rock to another. Assuming that I had seen the last of it, I continued my aesthetic study of plants bareheaded. Scarcely ten minutes had passed when all at once there appeared before me a

mountain-girl, who with rustic charm and a little embarrass-
ment handed me my poor hat. I thanked her warmly and
scanned her face. She was probably about sixteen or seventeen. Her face was tanned but her fresh, pink colouring
showed beneath her tan. Her remarkably white and even
teeth sparkled in her small mouth. There was a certain
element of reserve and curiosity in her eyes, a somewhat
impertinent shyness.

'Are you from Garbe, young lady?'

'No, sir, I'm from Idro.'

'And are you staying here?'

'I'm leaving tomorrow with my father, who's down
there in the scrub with our goats. Do you see him? Look
hard, over there.' And she pointed to the place, but I could
only just discern a man with a white beard, in the distance.

'Where do you live in Idro?'

'About two miles outside the village, on the road to
Mount Pinello.'

'And what's your name, pretty lass?'

'Terese, if you please, sir.'

We went on talking. I besieged her with questions, and
kept staring at her. Embarrassed by my scrutiny, her eyes
wandered here and there, occasionally meeting my gaze –
indeed, going straight to my heart. I had never thought of
marriage. I would laugh and swear with wide-eyed sincerity that I didn't know what love was.

She said that she had no one in the world but her father,
who adored her, and not for one day had he ever left her
on her own since she was born. But now the good old
man had to go to Gardegno for two weeks, to establish his
claim to the legacy of a brother who had died with
considerable assets but no offspring. Formerly a corporal
under the Austrians, the old man could read and write as
well as any lawyer, and was a person of some standing; he
was, besides, more agile, more energetic, and more plucky
than a young man of twenty. While her father was away,
the young girl was to remain in Idro, entrusted to the care
of her seventy-year-old godmother.

Doctor, as you can imagine, I went and stayed for two weeks in that clean, isolated little inn at Idro. Every morning and evening I climbed the steep, winding path strewn with sharp stones that led to Mount Pinello, and I would stop at the kind mountain-girl's house. For two days she said no. Then there wasn't a grassy nook on those precipitous slopes where she would not lie talking: in the daytime, seeking out the coolest shade beside a little stream, or in some natural cave, or in the spacious crevices among the huge boulders that had come hurtling down from the mountain-peaks, heaven knows when; and in the evening, during the early hours of darkness, seeking out some soft turf beneath the starry sky.

Terese was not of course like city girls: her skin was rough, her passion almost feral. For the first few days there were three things that she loved: her father, her goats, and me. After a week she did not speak any more of her father, and no longer looked after her goats. She would be waiting for me at the cottage door as soon as it was dawn. Often she came as far as Idro to meet me. She would drag me along, and use me with violence, and throw me to the ground as though she would tear me to pieces. Sometimes her body had a bitter, heady smell of wild herbs, and sometimes a foul smell of goats, and not infrequently a stench of mucky hay. In short, I longed for the old man's return.

The day before his arrival I tried to prepare Terese for my departure. I told her I had to go to Brescia and Milan, but I hastily added that I would be back soon, in two weeks' time at most, perhaps a week. She did not cry. She trembled all over, and turned the colour of lead. She kept saying in a choked voice, 'I know you won't come back, I know you won't come back.' I promised, I swore that I would, but she continued to stare at me dry-eyed, and with the clear-sightedness of passion she insisted, 'You won't come back. I sense, here in my heart, that you won't come back.' I couldn't get any other words out of her.

Instead of going to Brescia and Milan, I returned to

Garbe. Remorse gnawed at my soul: there were so many times when I felt pricked by conscience to go running back to Idro, to Terese's cottage. Then her wild, desperate embraces would scare me, and yet I couldn't think of anything else but her. I didn't know whether I loved her, although her image haunted me the whole time. Finally, after some four weeks, my conscience triumphed, and perhaps my curiosity. I went to Idro, making my way across poor meadows, clambering over rocks, and climbing up a dry riverbed, until I found myself in front of the cottage, on the other side of the path. I was hidden by trees and bushes.

The young girl was sitting in the doorway, not moving, unprotected from the rays of the sun. At first I did not recognize her: her complexion had turned dark red, while her matted hair fell over her forehead and shoulders in rat-tails; her face looked strangely long and thin, and her lower lip hung loosely; her lustreless eyes stared, unseeing, in front of her. I don't know why, I felt that I was in the presence of a withered corpse. At that moment a man's voice called out from inside the cottage, sounding so suppressed and sinister it seemed to come from a tomb: Terese, Terese. The girl gave no sign of having heard, and that dismal, harrowing voice kept calling: 'Terese, Terese.'

I fled. I went rushing off to Brescia, but I found the noise of the city intolerable. I returned to Garbe, where, after telling myself again and again that time heals all wounds, including the torments of passion and abandonment, I found a few moments' peace. Nevertheless, I did not get much sleep, afflicted as I was by terrible nightmares and feverish anxieties. I ate very little. I walked a great deal, hoping to tire myself out.

So, as I was telling you, doctor, on 24th October last, I was crossing the Ponte dei Re at Garbe, at nightfall. A man with his elbows resting on the parapet, holding his chin in his hands, was staring very intently at the water. Strands of a very white beard showed through his fingers. It was hard to see his face, which was half hidden by a hat pulled down over his brow. He was not exactly dressed as a peasant, nor as a worker. He wore a cloak and wide-legged trousers of a light greyish colour. I went past the old man. He did not stir. He continued to stare into the furiously swirling waters by the bridge pier, where the river is forced to pass through two arches. I too looked down, thinking there was something strange to see; I detected nothing out of the ordinary, but I liked the way the water surged, which I had never noticed before.

There was a tremendous battle between the onrushing river and the huge stones that tried to bar its way. And what efforts the river has to make, what cunning it must adopt, and how it has to toil to win its way forward, as these waters are pursued by the waters behind, and those chased on by yet more distant waters, all the way back to the rivulets that spring up amid the clouds.

The sight of the inexorable conflict between movement and immobility, eternally perpetuated each moment, is vaguely disheartening, and at the same time such blind impetuosity and such stubborn resistance makes one smile. There are moments when opposing forces of nature are like ill-brought up children, one of whom shouts 'I will', and the other stamps its foot and cries, 'You won't.'

And growing upon those rocks that stick up out of the riverbed amid those unquiet waters are young willow trees and poplar saplings, seeded by the wind in a handful of soil that has been deposited on those rocks one grain at a time by that very same wind. These weak and pliant plants are made to sing by the fury that surrounds them.

Nature, like life, is an endless series of bad jokes. If the rock does not raise its head very high, the water flows over it, and then falls in lively cascades, trying to reach the bottom: it is a clear and even, curved sheet of crystal, a limpid bell-jar, a transparent canopy, with a few opaque threads of Murano glass in it. And where it falls it shatters into a spray of tiny white pearls, of the kind that the women of Murano thread as they sit on their doorsteps on summer evenings, gossiping about Tita and Nane.

The water is clever: it usually chooses the best route. But sometimes it finds itself trapped among the stones, and then, unable to wait, it bursts into spray and races on. And sometimes it goes chasing round this way and that in a labyrinth, and in order to escape it has to retreat. One final thing that occurs is that it strays into an area where fate has placed an insurmountable stone obstacle, and then it stops, cowed, loses its sense of direction, acknowledges defeat and from turbulence turns to calm.

And beneath the water, which mirrors the colours of the sky in iridescent reflections, or turns into silver foam, there are the bold and varied colours of the rocks – yellow, red, white, moss and lichen-green.

The great battle is concentrated round the bridge pier. Water strives against water, in conflict with itself, crashing, smashing, massing and gathering, maddened with bellicose fury, producing foam instead of blood, and splashing spray up on to the bridge's parapet with a roar so mighty as to make a hero tremble.

The old man still stared down impassively.

I continued slowly on my way to Nozza, without concerning myself about him. The cloudy, storm-threatening sky was beginning to darken, and a cold wind blew down from the mountains. I decided not to go any further and turned back. The old man was still there, on the Ponte dei Re, in the same place, in the same position as before. He was still staring at the foot of the pier. The whole business seemed strange to me. I went up to the old man and said, 'Forgive me, my good fellow.'

He did not stir.

I went on. 'Forgive me for disturbing you, but the sky is black, there's a storm brewing, and it's almost dark. If you live some distance from here you should be on your way.'

The old man straightened up very slowly, looked into my face as though in a trance, and without a word returned to leaning on the parapet, gazing into the river.

I pressed him. 'Do you need anything?'

'No,' he answered without turning round.

I said goodnight and set off towards Garbe. I went a hundred yards and looked back. I don't know whether it was out of curiosity or compassion: I thought I had seen in that old man's face a profound sorrow, a fearful melancholy. With his sunken eyes, pallid complexion and dark lips, he had roused in me both pity and terror. I found myself at his side, driven by an almost involuntary force, and I said to him, brokenly, waiting for a reply that did not come, 'Forgive me again. Tell me if I can do anything for you. Are you not feeling very well? Let me offer you a room in Garbe for tonight. I take it you're a stranger here. I, too, have happened to find myself away from home with no money: perhaps you are in need of some?'

Whereupon the old man gravely turned round, trying to work his lips into a smile. 'No, thank you. I'm not in any need,' he replied. Then he dug his hand into his pocket and drew out a closed fist; then holding it over the parapet, he opened his hand. Some twenty little banknotes were caught by the wind and blown down into the river, scattered here and there.

As I was about to reprove him angrily, he stammered in a faint voice, 'I'm thirsty.'

'Go down and drink from the river!' I exclaimed harshly.

The old man walked to the flight of steps that descended on one side at the end of the bridge. But having got there, he swayed unsteadily on his feet. I ran to help him, and gripping him under the arm led him down to the river. It was I who filled his hat with water, which he drank in little sips.

'Don't put your wet hat back on your head, you'll catch a chill. Do you live far away?'

'No.'

'But you're not from this village?'

'No.'

'Where are you staying? I'll walk back with you.'

'There's no need. I've not far to go.'

'I'll come with you anyway.'

The old man looked me right in the eye and in a determined voice he said, 'I don't want you to.'

Then he added, less curtly, almost reluctantly, 'I'm waiting for someone.'

'A son, perhaps?'

'I have no children.'

'A relative?'

'I have no relatives.'

'A friend?'

'I have no friends.'

'Who then?'

He thought for a while, and replied, 'Destiny.'

He leant on the parapet again, and went back to staring into the water below.

'Forgive me for pressing you, but where are you from?'

'From a place where a person may die of sorrow.'

'And where are you going?'

'To a place I don't know.'

These mysterious answers awakened in my mind some foolish suspicion. I exclaimed effusively, 'If you have to remain in hiding, if the law is after you, I swear I shan't betray you.'

The old man drew himself up and replied in quite a different manner, 'No, I have nothing to hide from other men.' Then, murmuring to himself, he said, 'My conscience is clear.'

'Perhaps someone has tricked you, or done you harm? You've found many enemies in the world?'

'Enemies? I have only one.'

These last words were uttered by the old man in such a hollow voice, with such a sinister look in his eye that my blood ran cold.

'I'll leave you then, and God bless you.'

'God! God!' I heard him say several times. And the old man's sepulchral voice was drowned by the warring Chiese.

I did not mean to abandon the poor fellow. I reached

Garbe in no time, with the intention of talking to the mayor, a good doctor with a heart of gold, and of taking two villagers with me to stand guard, perhaps all night, over the strange old man. I found the mayor beneath the portico of his house, an old house built by one of his ancestors, a French nobleman who had fled the St Bartholomew Massacre.

The mayor was in conversation with the town clerk and the keeper of the inn at Sabbio, both odd characters. The publican is round-faced, large, and fat, with a long, thick, Vandyke beard and a big black moustache, fearsome eyebrows, a thundering voice, and a wide-brimmed hat on his head – all that's missing is the feather and he could pass for a Spaniard. Familiar with everybody, expansive, hail-fellow-well-met, he will place a protective arm on any man's shoulders – be he lawyer, chemist, or local bigwig – and readily opens his big mouth to laugh coarsely while telling some smutty joke. He's a kind of hidalgo, who grandly pours the wine from the jug into his guests' glasses; who holds his hand on his hip, amazed to find no sword there; who consumed his small inheritance within a few months, in order to acquire a taste for looking like a wholesale trader; and who hopes to take himself off to a big city worthy of him, far from the smallness of life in the mountains, where he really feels out of place.

The other fellow, the town clerk, is as tall and thin as Garbe's bell-tower. He dresses peasant-style, in a jacket and trousers made of that shiny, dark cinnamon-coloured material, but with the jacket thrown over his shoulders, revealing a shirt that doesn't always look clean, with his arms and chest bare, and very much darker than his clothes. He has read Dante, writes like a very educated person, knows by heart all the numerous directives and countless prefectorial circulars sent to the Town Hall, which is a miraculous achievement. He quotes Latin verses and proverbs. He has no house; in winter he sleeps on the bare surface of the Town Council table, with a bust from the archives for a pillow and the green baize cloth for a cover. In the summer he sleeps beneath the little portico of that church of San Gottardo I mentioned earlier, resting his head on the granite step, stretched out on the uneven flagstones, enjoying the cool breeze that blows constantly from the narrow neck of the valley. He lives on bread and onions, and polenta and cheese made of ewe's milk, but he compensates himself with the odd glass of aquavit, and when he has drunk a little more than he needs, he tries to embrace everybody, including the mayor and even the carabinieri on duty.

These gentlemen, and three villagers I went and flushed out of the nearby tavern, set off for the bridge with me. We passed by the church of San Gottardo, the town clerk's summer residence, but when we got there I could not restrain myself any more: I left the elderly mayor to continue at his own pace – he, poor fellow, was trying to speed up but still seemed to me too slow – and I ran on ahead. I went back and forth across the bridge. I rushed down the steps to the river. I peered here and there into the darkness of the night that had now fallen: there was not a soul to be seen. The others joined me, out of breath. I lost no time in giving them instructions: the mayor was to stay on the bridge, the hidalgo was to take the search half a kilometre along the road to Nozza; the clerk was to go back up the Chiese, following a path on the left. The three villagers were to climb the less steep of the mountain paths – as for the more precipitous ones, it was out of the question that the old man could have attempted them. Rendezvous: on the bridge.

I had reserved for myself the charcoal-burners' huts on the far side of the river. In fifteen minutes I had climbed up to the first cottage. Everyone was asleep. I knocked loudly: no one answered. I hammered again so hard that the noise resounded in the valley, and at last I heard voices and cursing. After a short while the little window opened and I saw a black face in which two little eyes gleamed like a cat's.

'Do you know anything about an old man with a long

white beard who's far from well, and dressed in light-coloured clothes, a stranger who was wandering about by the Ponte dei Re this evening?'

'Go to hell.'

'Please, ask your companions about it.'

'Go to hell, both you and the old man.' And he closed the window.

A quarter of an hour later I had already retraced my steps and climbed up to another hut in the other direction. When I banged my stick on the little wooden door it echoed four or five times among the mountaintops.

'Who is it?'

'A friend.'

'Name?'

'A friend.'

'I'm not opening the door.'

'Come to the window.'

'I'm not moving.'

'Have you seen an old man?'

'I've not seen anybody.'

'A sick old man with a long white beard, in light-coloured clothing.'

'I haven't seen anybody.'

'He was on the Ponte dei Re this evening, and walking on the paths nearby.'

'I've not seen anybody, I tell you.' And there was a sound of snoring again.

Three-quarters of an hour later we were all on the bridge. We had found nothing and learned nothing. Not even the two carabinieri from Vestone that the hidalgo had met on the road and brought back with him, were able to help in any way. The mayor then decided that we should all go and get some sleep. It was indeed the only sensible thing to do.

My dear doctor, I've told you what a treasure this mayor of ours is. He has his very own way of treating diphtheria, thanks to which he really does save all the children in the community. He talks about his remedies

179

with youthful enthusiasm: they never fail. An inflammation requires blood-letting, indeed every ailment poisons the blood and drawing off the bad blood allows healthy blood to develop. Now he lives a fairly trouble-free existence, looking after his two fields. But for thirty years he was the local doctor, and when he recalls the long, badly paid hours he used to work, the intense heat, the snow, the freezing cold, and the storms in the mountains, he does so with such fondness he almost seems to regret it all. He's always ready to to talk with affectionate sympathy about his patients, and if he can say that he saved them from death, two tears of joy roll down his cheeks. He has a grey beard, and slightly grizzled hair, very white teeth, blue eyes and the brow of a virtuous and intelligent man. He takes snuff, and offers it to others. Every year he says he doesn't want to be mayor any more; then he makes the same mistake again. He can't say no. Good or bad, everybody respects and loves him.

I've never heard him say a bitter, or sharp, or harsh word about anyone, were he the most wicked villain. There's not the least trace of animosity in that soul of his, even towards homeopathy, which says it all. He talks with great naturalness about the humble circumstances of his life, when as a student at Padua University, with only one zwanger a day to his name, he would have old rice served to him at the inn because it cost a few cents less, and bones of beef stripped of flesh, and the ends of salames. He never drank wine. One day, having seen a conjurer performing in the Piazza dei Signori, he made friends with him, and dined with him several times, until he had learned the secret of his magic, thinking that, if medicine failed him, this other art might come to his rescue. He told an endless series of stories, some to make you happy, others that were terrifying.

Now at last I must come to the heart of my story. You will have noticed my reluctance to do so. In fact I realize that with all this scribbling down on paper I've been behaving like a person with toothache who goes to have it pulled out. He goes rushing off, almost running, but as he gradually approaches the dentist's surgery he begins to drag his feet, and when he gets to the door he stops, perplexed, asking himself, 'Is my tooth hurting now or not?'

And then he turns round and retraces his steps for quite some way. And every little thing serves as an excuse for delay – a notice on a street corner, a barking dog. Then, ashamed of himself, he marches up to the door, feeling determined, and with his hand already poised to ring the bell, again he asks himself, 'Should I have it pulled out or not?'

Well, to continue then. That evening, having given the three villagers money to buy a few jugfuls, and having said goodbye to the mayor, who was going home, and to the clerk, who was going to wish the liquor distiller a goodnight, and the hidalgo, who was returning to Sabbio, singing to himself in his bass voice, I had no desire to sleep, or even to write, read, or talk. I felt a great weight bearing down on my head, and I needed to get some fresh air, to draw the biting wind deep into my lungs.

There had been an interminable discussion in the inn a few evenings back on whether the trout fishing between Vestone and Vobarno was better at nightfall or early in the morning, on a moonlit night or a dark night. One fisherman swore that he would land a huge catch in pitch darkness.

I took my fishing rod and a small lamp, and went and positioned myself on the far side of the Chiese, where some enormous rocks form a kind a dam. Every now and again, thinking there was something biting, I would bring the line up: nothing. Feeling bored, I sat down on a stone and looked round. It was impossible to see anything at all. The sky was black, and so was the ground: there was not a single star, or light. Garbe, which lay hidden behind a clump of trees, was sleeping at that hour. Up on the mountainridge, just where Proviligio must have been, appeared a glimmer of light, perhaps a candle at someone's deathbed. It was as dark as a tomb, but a tomb full of noise. The Chiese battering against the rocks made a deafening roar that encompassed every pitch, every timbre of sound, to which the wind added the shrillest of notes. Little by little, as my eyes eventually adapted to the darkness, I was able to make out a few things: the big ugly toads jumping sideways close by me, the white foam and the dark green of the water.

I had picked up my rod to try my luck again, when I saw a large, light-coloured mass come hurtling downstream until it was stopped by the dam. I did not know what it was, and yet a shudder ran through me from head to foot. I picked up my lamp, which I had left on the path, but as I approached that grey object with the lamp, the water that had been seething round it, lifted it up and carried it twenty yards further downstream, where it slammed against a big stone sticking up out of the river. Straining to see sharpened my vision. Aided by the pale glimmer of the lamp, I tried to ford that small stretch of water, using the rocks as stepping stones. I did not succeed. I stood there, motionless, staring.

The water drove against the shapeless mass, spewing foam as though enraged, and surged round it, creating a fast-swirling eddy. The Chiese furiously persisted in its determination to sweep its prey on. It had its way. The strange object cleared the rock and continued on its course, violently tossed about by the river.

Then began a terrific battle between myself, who wanted to know the mystery of that light-coloured object, and the river that wanted to withhold it from me. I know every inch of the paths along the riverbank. There is just one place where the rockface rises almost vertically for some one hundred metres, forcing you to climb up and then down. The rest of the way to Sabbio, it's flat. But that climb and especially that descent, at night, along a narrow ledge with the ravine on one side, were not without danger.

182

The rain of the past few days had caused the land to fall away from the path at one point, and you had to leap across a precipice. I leapt without thinking, not knowing where I would land, and found myself safe and sound on the other side, but the lamp had blown out. I continued along the goat-path in the dark, stumbling over scrub, hedged round by thorny bushes, sliding down the slope, slipping on the round pebbles that went rolling to the bottom. At last I got to the riverbank again. But where was the grey mass? Had it gone racing on ahead, unimpeded, or had the obstacles with which the Chiese abounds checked its progress? I waited for a moment without blinking, my eyes getting so dry they smarted. Eventually it came flashing past in an instant.

And I, too, was off again, racing along that part of the riverbank where the slender willows and broad-leafed water-lilies start. The meadow above there is green, dotted with flowers, and as well as poplars there are pines, elms, and a few little oak trees. I had often sat down there on a tree-stump, studying the ants, admiring the golden-yellow, ruby-red and emerald-green insects, reading a good book or daydreaming on frivolous matters amid the emptiness of life. A little further on, where the path skirts a field of stunted corn-cobs, I had lain back one morning to watch for a whole hour three young women collecting walnuts. Shaken down from a tree by a boy, the nuts fell into the river and the three laughing women had their skirts hitched up round their hips with their fat legs showing to above the knee.

The grey mass had run aground on a bank of gravel close to the riverside. I took off my socks and shoes and waded into the water. I could not stand on my feet. The river kept bringing me down with insuperable violence. I was aware of the littleness of man before the will of insensate forces. At that moment the Chiese must have summoned to its aid all the forces in its depths; a surge of water covered the gravel-bank, engulfing the horrible grey object, which was then carried inexorably on. I felt defeated.

I returned to my room in Garbe, exhausted, soaking wet and drenched in sweat. My eyes were swollen, my head was burning, my pulse was racing. I could not sleep. As soon as it was light I staggered out of bed and went to Sabbio, taking the postal track along the left bank of the Chiese. At times my limbs were freezing cold, at times I had to wipe my brow.

At Sabbio, where I often went for breakfast, the hidalgo and his publican wife greeted me with great kindness, asking me a dozen times whether I was ill. 'It's nothing,' I replied. 'The fresh air, the walk and breakfast will set me to rights.' I didn't eat a thing. I stared as if in a trance at the big shed draped with cobwebs, the hens that came pecking at the crumbs of polenta to carry them back to their chicks, at the church of Our Lady, standing high on the hill just close by, looking as though it was stuck on top of the roof of the inn.

While I sat there, lost in a dream, Pierino, one of the landlady's sons, a fine sturdy boy of seven, came in, and started shouting, 'Mama, have you seen him?'

'Who?'

'The man they found in the river this morning.'

'Is he handsome?'

'No, he's very ugly. Ask Nina.'

Nina had come in with her brother, but she had immediately crept into a corner of the shed with her hands joined, murmuring something under her breath. At intervals I heard the word 'requiem', subdued and mournful.

'Is he young or old?' asked their mother.

Nina did not reply. Pierino answered, 'He's old, with a very long white beard. He has staring eyes.'

'Where is he? I want to see him,' I cried, springing to my feet.

The landlady eyed me, and murmuring, 'My God, the things that please some people!' she told Pierino to go with me.

In no time we had reached the church, the one down at the bottom of the village. The drowned man's body was laid out in a damp room next to the sacristy. The room was packed with villagers.

One said, 'Who's going to identify him? It's obvious from his clothes that he's not from here.'

Another added, 'I say he's German.'

'No, he's from Milan.'

'Didn't they find anything on him?' asked a young fellow.

'Nothing: no papers, no money.'

'He must have drowned himself, out of misery.'

'I say he fell into the river.'

'I say he was thrown in.'

'Those eyes look demonic.'

'With his mouth open like that, he looks as though he would eat us alive.'

A child cowered behind her father, trembling, and said, 'I'm scared, let's go.'

The father, meanwhile, after taking a close look at the drowned man's coat and fingering the material, gave his verdict: 'Good cloth. It must have cost him a bit.'

I pushed my way through the crowd. The old man from the Ponte dei Re was staring into my face with sinister, menacing eyes. I detected the utmost censure in that fixed gaze. A sepulchral murmur rang in my ears: 'You left me to die, damn you. You could have saved me. You left me to die, damn you. You guessed what I was about to do, and you left me to die, damn you.'

The ceiling weighed down on my head, the crowd pressed round me. I felt as though I were in hell, surrounded by devils, being judged by a grey corpse's cavernous voice and implacable eyes.

A villager came in, a fellow I had seen in Idro. At the sight of the drowned man, he exclaimed, 'Poor old man! He loved her so dearly! He could only survive two days after his Terese died.'

I went to bed with a raging fever. An emotional morning, the exhaustion of the night before, and my feelings of remorse had their effect: I suffered terrible hallucinations. My eyes were very sore. The kindly mayor came to see me twice a day, and spent long hours at my bedside, administering medicine to me himself, and when he thought I looked a little calmed, quietly recounting a few anecdotes, which failed to make me laugh.

Gradually the fever abated, but even with quinine it didn't go away. The doctors say that it is one of those recurrent fevers brought on again by dampness or exhaustion. I quietly endure it. But I can in no way tolerate this accursed blotch in my eyes. No sooner had I recovered from my delirium than it was there before me, and I see it still, as I have described to you, a persistent abomination . . .

Even now, there's a vague, colourless shape wobbling in front of me, fouling the white page. The sun has already set, and my writing desk is in shadow; it's light enough to dash down these words on paper, but not to re-read them. I wanted to finish this before putting on the light, and the blotch takes advantage of the semi-darkness to torment my mind.

The blotch is getting bigger, and − this is something new − it's taking on the shape of a man. It's sprouting arms, and legs, it's growing a head. It's that old man, that terrible old man!

I'm leaving tonight. I shall give you this manuscript myself, tomorrow. I'll either be cured, or I'll tear my eyes out.

BUDDHA'S COLLAR

Gioacchino certainly had something on his mind that was bothering him. He sat down, planting his elbows on the table and resting his thin cheeks on his bony hands, and lowered his eyelids as though about to ponder at length on some serious misfortune. But after a minute he leapt to his feet, went to the small tarnished mirror on the chest of drawers, and stared with a troubled gaze at his glum reflection. Seeing that he looked sallower than usual (he had not slept a wink all night), he felt a shudder run through him from head to foot. Then he took his pulse, thinking he had a temperature.

The window was wide open, but although not yet seven in the morning it was terribly hot. The mercilessly bright, July sun that blazed down on the little street only a metre or so wide had turned the paving into a strip of fiery white, so that when the young man went and stood at the window, he felt blinded. Gradually adapting to the light, he settled his gaze on the crooked bridge at the end of the street, and on the lovely greenness of Venice's canals that is so restful to the eyes. And Gioacchino was, indeed, momentarily calmed by the sight of that beautiful, shimmering emerald.

Down in the street, Zaccaria was sitting under the shade of a patched red awning. In his shop, a pair of red shoes was displayed beside a shiny, copper bowl that was all embossed, like the huge, gleaming plates in Zamaria's pancake stall. Next to a pair of mended trousers and a rusty spear were a sword with a gilded hilt, the legacy of a member of Austria's Aulic Council, and a snuff-box with a few merry little cupids painted on it a century ago by a French miniaturist.

Gioacchino called down from the fourth floor, 'Zaccaria!'

Zaccaria looked up, raising the two points of his grey beard.

The young man asked hoarsely, 'Did anyone come?'

The other shrugged his shoulders and looked down again.

Back in the dimness of his room, Gioacchino had started to examine some sort of heavy, white-metal collar, four fingers wide, on which were engraved in Gothic characters the three letters FAQ, and he rubbed away at it with a cloth. A thought occurred to him that cheered him: the collar might be made of silver.

He hurriedly got dressed. His detachable collar and cuffs were freshly starched and laundered, though his shirt was rather grubby; but his black jacket looked new and apparently tailor-made for our Gioacchino's gangly frame. The only thing that spoiled the effect was the way his boots, which came to just below the knee, showed under his light trousers. These boots, inherited from an uncle, were decidedly too big for his thin legs, and must have been extremely uncomfortable in the summer heat.

Anyway, Gioacchino went out, with the collar in his hand, and a hundred yards from his house entered a very small, low-ceilinged shop with a few brass clocks in the window, some huge, silver pocket-watches, five or six neck-chains, and a few pairs of dubious gold ear-rings. Stepping into the shop, he could not see anything at all – it was pitch black. But gradually his eyes began to distinguish things. In one corner, where a bit of weak light came in, was an old man with glasses on his nose who was examining through a magnifying-glass the workings of a broken clock.

'Oh, Signor Gioacchino! It's been a long time since I've seen you! Have you something for me to buy?'

'No. I want to ask you a favour.'

'Willingly. As long as it's not money. Even if seven of my teeth were pulled out – the way that King of England tried to extract money from a Jew – I wouldn't part with a single lire for the eighth. Not that I have seven teeth in my head, anyway. And besides, you've plenty of teeth and money to lend everybody, Signor Gioacchino. Now, how can I be of service to you?'

'Take a look at this.'

The old man glanced at the metal object and said at once, 'It's silver, pure, solid silver.'

'What would it be worth?'

'Do you want to sell it?'

'No, I said I didn't.'

'Well, let's weigh it. That would be about thirty lire — less rather than more. Did you find this collar?'

'Yes.'

'I didn't think it belonged to any dog of yours. I have the impression,' he said, with a sardonic glance at the young fellow's outsized boots, 'that you don't much care for dogs. Neither did your late uncle.'

As the jeweller-cum-clockseller mumbled these words, shaking with laughter, a young ragamuffin went past, crying out in a high-pitched voice, '*Adriatico! Adriatico!* All the latest news stories . . .'

Gioacchino hastily thanked the old man and ran after the boy to buy a newspaper, then he carried it up to his room, taking the steps three at a time up the extremely narrow staircase. He scoured the bottom of page three, and found, printed in large letters, the notice that had already appeared in all the previous day's papers: '*Whoever has lost a dog-collar with three initials on it, the first of which is F, is invited to come and collect it as soon as possible at the shop called the Golden Shield, at number 512 in Calle della Forca. Upon identification of the other two letters, the collar will be handed over without any reward demanded.*'

There were two or three typographical errors, but all in all the text was clear.

Eight o'clock sounded. The young man went rushing out again, pushed hard against the door two or three times to make sure it was properly closed. As he passed by the Golden Shield he said to Zaccaria, who was still sitting under the red awning, 'So we're agreed: if anyone comes asking for the collar, send them to the cashier at the Commercial Assurance Bank. All right?'

'I know, I know. You told me the same thing a hundred times yesterday.'

'Well, I rely on you then.'

And from his position in the shade of that little street from which the sun had now left, Zaccaria stared after Gioacchino as he crossed the bridge almost running. 'It's strange how all of a sudden he's become obsessed with returning the thing to its owner,' he murmured under his breath. 'I'd never have believed it!'

Meanwhile, Gioacchino was thinking, 'It's silver. The owner will come running to collect it.'

It is important to know that Gioacchino was not at all miserly. But the antiques dealer at the Golden Shield was right: this obsession of his was decidedly eccentric. The young man, as we shall see, spent everything he earned. His room could not be described as dirty, although Zaccaria's grumbly wife dusted the chest of drawers, mirror, four chairs, sagging armchair and wormeaten table only once every two weeks. The furniture was Gioacchino's personal property; he paid five lire a month for the unfurnished room and one lire a month for the services of Zaccaria's good lady, which was a great deal more than she deserved. Then there was his food, clothing and entertainment: that came to three lire a day, not a cent more nor less. Gioacchino had inherited from his saintly uncle one hundred thousand lire, or thereabouts, and his handling of these funds as cashier of the Assurance Bank had, at the last statement of account, brought him a net income of ten thousand lire, which was to double the following year. But this was not what he himself earned, it was what his money earned – an important distinction. Gioacchino had, among other virtues, that of modesty: he did not rate his own work very highly. And after much intensive calculation, his thirteen-hour day, from eight in the morning until six in the evening, and from eight in the evening until eleven at night, had seemed to him to be worth only three lire a day. So his income was equal to his outgoings. However, he occasionally suspected himself of being a reckless fellow at heart, and then he would cut down a little on his expenses, so that from his own actual earnings he had saved about one hundred lire, plus a few cents, with which he could afford to be wildly extravagant once in a while. It is no bad thing for a provident young man to build up a reserve of cash, like this, that he can draw on in the last resort, to pay for some whim or other.

The time for such an extravagance – a real and unforeseen extravagance – had arrived. Gioacchino's ideas about women were very sentimental. Those who expected to be paid he did not find attractive, but on the other hand those who did not expect to be paid did not seem to find Gioacchino very attractive. The problem with unattached young girls was the over-enthusiasm, and often the troublesomeness, of their brothers or fathers. As for married women, Gioacchino's moral principles – and to a small extent his fear of their cantankerous husbands – banished them from his thoughts. And so our young hero, who was as thin as a rake, with his pale, sallow face, small, dark eyes, thick, purple lips, sparse, goatee beard, sunken cheeks and almost bald head, lived a fretfully chaste life.

At six thirty one evening, as he was coming out of his Bank into the Merceria di San Salvatore, a splendid-looking young woman went by. She was tall and slender, with raven hair, and big, black eyes that gave him gooseflesh, and the warm, brown glow of her complexion (she wore a slightly plunging neckline) seemed to reflect an inward ardour. Gioacchino felt his heart miss a beat, and having gone two paces, he looked back. At exactly the same moment, the beautiful young woman also turned round, flashing her big, black eyes.

When she had gone some distance, an irresolute, trembling Gioacchino plucked up the courage to follow her. If he lost sight of her at the bend in one of the little streets, or going over a bridge, he quickened his step, running to catch up. Then when she came into view again, he would stop dead, and if she lingered in front of a shop for a moment, looking in the window, he would go and hide furtively in a dark passageway. He tried to walk non-chalantly, whistling and gazing into the air. He alternated between fear and boldness: three or four times he felt the urge to accost the girl: he would take a couple of steps towards her, and lose heart. And so they went through San Bartolomeo, over the Ponte dell'Olio, then along Salizzada di San Giovanni Grisostomo, and finally came to Campo dei Santi Apostoli, where his enchantress met an old woman dressed in black, wearing a little hat with pink flowers.

It was blazing hot in the large square, which still lay in sunshine. The girl and the old woman turned the corner into Calle del Pistor, and disappeared in Ramo delle Zotte, where the green waters of a canal could be seen glinting at the end of the alleyway, with the cabin of a black gondola gliding past.

To cut a long story short, five days later the fat, wrinkled, little old woman in the rose-trimmed hat had already with great cunning got our prudent young fellow to part with forty lire of his available funds.

Irene was truly a goddess of seduction. When she stood at full height, Gioacchino's half-bald pate only came up to her oval-shaped chin. But she stooped so gracefully! She was like a panther in the way that she bounded forward, and the way her body flexed and swayed; and she had the slinky sinuousness of a snake. And besides she was so high-spirited. Her upper lip remained naturally upturned, especially at the corners, in an adorable curve that put one slightly in mind of a dog, and always revealed her very white teeth. Her incisors must have been as sharp as knife-blades, and her canines were surely as pointed as daggers. It suited her so well to laugh: her eyes sparkled with what seemed a wild quiver of gaiety.

Gioacchino had lost his head. He would go over to Calle delle Zotte straight after he had eaten and stay there until a quarter to eight, when it was time for him to return to the bank. He would have gone there during the day as well, had he been able to get away from the bank, even for ten minutes. He would have returned there late at night if the young lady and her old mother had not forbidden it, telling him that they always went to bed extremely early, and they had no intention of putting their reputation as honest women at risk in the neighbourhood. The fact is that a week after their first encounter, the old woman extracted another thirty lire from the young man. But Irene loved him so much, and threw herself at him with such passion, he was enchanted! And she had the charming habit of giving him little bites; when Gioacchino undressed at night he examined the marks on his own flesh with infinite gratification.

One afternoon (they had known each other for nine days) the girl was even more lively and Gioacchino more inflamed than usual.

Irene suddenly cried, 'I want to show you once and for all how much I love you!' And she came up to him, and taking him by the shoulder turned him round, and with those sharp, pointed teeth of hers gave him a big bite below the nape of his neck. 'Blood, blood!' she said repeatedly, hooting with laughter.

Although it hurt a little, and he was sorry to get his shirt-collar and neck-tie stained, pale, gaunt-faced Gioacchino laughed, too, and wiped the wound with a handkerchief.

It was almost eight o'clock. He left, a happy man, using his handkerchief at brief intervals to dab his neck, on which the drops of blood kept welling up again. Since it would not stop bleeding, he went into a chemist and had a bit of yellow plaster put on it. It felt sore during the night, which kept him awake.

The following evening Gioacchino was burning with love, although throughout the day he had felt a very great weariness in his every limb. The old woman was waiting for him as usual at the street door. When Gioacchino saw her, he whispered to himself, 'Here we go again!'

Sure enough, the old woman drew him into the kitchen, where two pots, a small kettle, five or six round plates and a few sets of rusted cutlery were displayed on the dresser. Then the lamentations began. Irene knew nothing about it, poor thing, but there were some very urgent debts, some insolent creditors to be kept quiet. Thirty lire would be enough. He was so good, so kind. She swore on the image of St Brigida that she would never trouble him again. Gioacchino remained unmoved.

Then the old woman planted her hands on her hips and, dispensing with the studied kindness of her wrinkled face and unnatural sweetness of her shrill voice, she continued shrewishly. Irene depended on her. It wasn't love that paid the bills. She should have kicked him in the pants and then closed the door in his face, for ever and ever, Amen. And what a face! If he wanted to continue to see her daughter, he, too, would have to contribute to the household expenses. After all, she was such a pure, innocent girl that he had all to himself. And besides, it was only a matter of a few lire. He was just being mean and petty. Anyway, who did he think he was dealing with? People should be valued at their worth, and she and her daughter wanted to be treated like respectable women. Was that clear?

Gioacchino handed over the last twenty-five lire. All that was left now of the savings on the salary he had allotted himself were a few miserable cents. But the young man was so ardently in love that he did not think that dipping into the twenty thousand lire that his investments were supposed to bring in that year, for another one hundred lire, was the worst thing in the world that could happen.

Irene was lying on the couch. The heat was oppressive, humid, and suffocating. She was dressed in a rather short slip and a robe with almost all the buttons undone. Gioacchino brightened up when he saw her. His little eyes widened, and his pallid face took on a good rosy colour.

He whispered in the young girl's ear those eternal words, 'Do you love me?'

She answered aloud, laughing, 'I adore you.'

'Am I the only one you love? Are you always thinking of me? You know I would give every drop of my blood for my beloved Irene.' And he gently chided her for the bite she had given him the previous evening, saying that his neck was still very sore.

He had laid his head in her lap. Lost in a kind of blissful stupor, he stared, unthinking, at the thick dust that had lain undisturbed for several months beneath the few sticks of furniture; at the griminess of the floor that would have scandalized even Zaccaria's good wife; and at the filth clinging to the curtains at the window. An acrid stench rose from the almost dry canal. Something white and shiny, behind one of the skewed legs of the wardrobe, caught Gioacchino's eye.

'Look, what's that under there?' he asked, and without waiting for a reply he went and picked up the object. It was a dog-collar, with a buckle and the three letters F.A.Q. on it.

Gioacchino's face turned pale. 'A dog? There's been a dog in this house? Answer me.'

Irene laughed, showing her teeth.

'There was a dog here, and it lost its collar? When?'

'Yesterday morning.'

'Yesterday?'

'Yes, yesterday.' And the young woman thought for a while and added, 'It came in from the stairs – in this heat, Mama always leaves the door open. But I'm not afraid of dogs. In fact, look!' And she pointed to two long, parallel flesh-wounds, close together in her right calf, which had not yet healed.

'It was the dog that did that?' cried Gioacchino, his eyes popping out of his head.

'Yes, it was the dog. I'd almost forgotten about it.'

'And you didn't have the wound cauterized?'

'You must be crazy! I'd be left with the scar for the rest of my life.'

'And where's the dog now?'

'I don't know! I'd never seen it before. It ran off, and good riddance to it.'

'It ran off straight away?'

'Straight away, and in such a frenzy it might have been rabid.'

Rabid! Rabid! And he touched the bite on his neck, which for the past minute had been burning his flesh like a hot coal. He put the collar in his pocket and fled, rushing down the stairs, racing through the streets, over bridges, along the canalside, pushing everyone out of his way, until he reached the Main Hospital, where he asked for the duty surgeon. He wanted to have himself treated with a hot iron and scalpel, but the surgeon said that nothing could be done now since the wound was already healed. Besides, having been informed of the circumstances, he categorically maintained that rabies was not transmitted between human beings, and telling Gioacchino that he need not lose any more sleep over it, he walked off.

Gioacchino thought, 'It's a lie, a white lie. I must know the truth.' And as he hurried home, he passed by the Santa Fosca Dispensary. Knowing the pharmacist, he went straight in. When he got to the counter, he sneezed. The air, which was filled with the smell of drugs, unguents and medicines, tickled the nerve-ends in his nose.

The Santa Fosca Dispensary is famous. Its miraculous pills on several occasions came to the attention of the Grand Council of the Republic of Venice, no less. It occupies a rather large room of very solemn appearance. A perfectly preserved survival of baroque art, it has big, heavy, wooden cupboards all the way round, with pilasters, cornices, pediments, elaborate panels and curved volutes. Over the door in the middle, opposite the entrance, is the bust of an elderly sage in the act of consulting an enormous pharmacopeical tome. Above the door on the right stands the bust of a young man holding a retort, and over the one of the left, that of another young man with a pestle and mortar. On top of the pediments are a number of allegorical, gilt figures of reclining women; with dolphins and caducei here and there. There is not a single cobweb on the ceiling, whose regular beams are painted with yellow flowers. On the shelves are white porcelain jars decorated with blue leaf-work, bearing inscriptions in black Gothic letters. The largest and most full-bellied jars stand on the top shelf, medium-sized ones on the middle shelf, and small ones below – a hand used to weighing out small amounts with scrupulous exactness is evident in the way the jars are all neatly lined up next to each other.

There were four doctors sitting round a table in the adjoining room, talking, whilst the pharmacist was busy behind the counter, weighing out and wrapping up goodness knows what white powders.

Ashamed to enquire about himself, Gioacchino began to describe to the pharmacist the case of a friend of his who had been bitten by a woman, who had in turn been bitten by a dog that was very likely rabid. As he went on, getting carried away with the details of the story, his voice got loud and louder, so the doctors were able to hear through the open doorway. The point that Gioacchino wished to be enlightened upon was this: could hydrophobia be transmitted between human beings?

The pharmacist did not know what to reply. However, in the meantime, an old woman came in asking for three ounces of castor-oil. Leading Gioacchino into the adjoining room, the pharmacist put his question to the doctors, with the old woman tugging at his coat-tails to make him hurry up and give her the laxative that was needed to cure her daughter-in-law of colic, for today being a fast-day, the daughter-in-law, a fine figure of a young woman, had eaten too much cod.

The four doctors, who had been waiting in vain for a client, and meanwhile did not know how to pass the time, thought this was a good question, but very complicated. One of the them, the oldest, recalled having read in the periodical *Experimental Medicine* of a case of hydrophobia being passed on to a little boy bitten by a little girl before it was apparent she had rabies. Gioacchino turned white. It was true that the story was later denied in the same periodical. Gioacchino breathed again.

Meanwhile, the second doctor, a beardless fellow with

long fair hair and spectacles, had started searching through the bookshelves that covered three sides of the room (the richest pharmaceutical library in Venice), and he had dug out the June 1880 issue of the *International Journal of Medical Science*. Abruptly interrupting his colleagues' discussions, he began to read out slowly and gravely from page 488 the following short article: 'On the Transmission of Rabies' by Dr Raynaud. 'Until now it had been considered indisputable that a person with rabies was not able to transmit the disease to other people. Today it appears that this matter has now reached a stage that is anything but reassuring. We may draw the conclusion from a number of experiments that the *virus rabidus* in man is contagious. The inoculation of rabbits with saliva or with scrapings taken from the saliva glands of a man infected with rabies after he had been bitten by an animal suspected of having the disease, had caused symptoms of rabies, and then death. From which we may deduce that rabies may be transmitted not only from human beings to animals, but also between human beings. And granted that this is so, it is clearly necessary to take the utmost care to guard against being bitten by patients suffering from rabies, and to beware of their saliva and of any objects that might be contaminated by it, especially in cases of cuts, scratches or sores on the hands.'

Gioacchino had turned as white and still as a corpse, apart from his trembling lips. But warming to their subject, the doctors paid no attention to him at all.

One of them, the youngest of the four, a small, hunched, little fellow with sharp eyes and tongue, remarked, 'That article is of no importance. Admittedly, men are like rabbits in terms of their character, but are not to be confused with them physically. I'm afraid to say, I know all about this. Hydrophobia was the subject of my doctoral thesis: I had to consult a mountain of books, and I had the help of Professor Lussana, who has conducted some major experiments. You surely remember poor Dr Agostino Marin, the general practitioner in Cervarese Santa Croce –

such a kind man, and so loved by everybody – who was bitten by a dog. When he began suffering the first symptoms of hydrophobia three months later, he took his horse and trap, and drove himself to Padua Hospital, where he calmly told the doctor on duty, 'I've come to die here, so as not to distress my wife and children, whom I love very dearly, with the dreadful spectacle of my death.' And indeed he did die a few days later, and Professor Lussana, who obtained a little of the unfortunate fellow's blood, injected it into the femoral veins of two dogs. One of the dogs died shortly afterwards, the other was put down. They had both been infected with the so-called *idrofobia lipemaniaca* or *taciturna*.'

The fair-haired doctor broke in. 'Well, then, if a human being can transmit rabies to rabbits and dogs, through saliva or blood, why not to another human being?'

'My dear doctor, why are horses, donkeys and cows subject to different diseases from those of the human species? Are there not some poisons that kill certain types of animals and have no effect whatsoever on others? Hertwig stated that only one in five of the men actually bitten by rabid dogs caught the disease: and Giraud, Bezard, Parvisse, Gauhier, Vaughan . . . '

'No more, please!' cried the pharmacist from the counter.

'. . . Giraud and Babington all inoculated themselves without ever contracting the least trace of hydrophobia. None of the courageous dissectors who cut or scratched their hands while examining the bodies of hydrophobics ever suffered anything at all, with one exception apparently, if Andry is to be believed.'

'The conclusion to be drawn is this,' said the old doctor. 'That we know nothing about it. But I admit that I wouldn't like to put it to the test and let a hydrophobic person sink his teeth into my flesh – not even if I were to be showered with gold.'

Gioacchino had collapsed onto a chair. He was listening, but no longer daring to breathe. He plucked up courage, and stammered out a question to the little hunch-backed doctor sitting next to him. 'Excuse me, is rabies always identifiable in men and dogs by their frenzy, their howling, the way they foam at the mouth, or by some other sure sign of the disease?'

Delighted to be able to show off his knowledge, the latter-day Aesculpius replied, 'No. Rabies does not manifest itself in fits of rage. In fact, in its early stages it's a disease that appears benign, but even from the beginning the patient's saliva is virulent – in other words, it contains the infectious germ. And a dog, or indeed a human being, is undoubtedly more dangerous during this stage when licking you with its tongue, than for any tendency to bite. A lot of foaming at the mouth is apparently not always evident. Sometimes the throat is wet, sometimes dry. In one particular form of the disease, called *rabbia muta*, the lower jaw becomes very disjointed from the upper jaw, and you can see right down into the animals black throat. Often the dog walks unsteadily, with its tail slack and head bowed, with staring eyes, and a long, bluish tongue hanging out of its mouth. It lifts its head to bite and then immediately reverts to its moribund demeanour.

'And has anyone come up with any other remedy since attempts to use curara proved unsuccessful?' asked the old doctor, who was no longer inclined to keep up with the dubious advances made in his science.

'Tracheotomy,' replied the hunchback.

'Tracheotomy,' Gioacchino murmured quietly. 'What's that?'

'It involves cutting into the trachea . . . ' And the doctor pointed to below his collar. 'The *pathos eminens* of hydrophobia consists of a laryingo-pharyngeal spasm. Since this obstructs breathing, the throat is cut open so that air can be drawn in below the obstruction.'

Gioacchino was filled with horror, but the doctor went on without looking at him. 'It's true that the patient eventually dies anyway, choking, epileptic, raging, foaming and bleeding at the mouth, and as in the case of *delirium tremens*, performing the most appalling dance of death.'

While his colleagues carried on their discussion, the fair-haired, bespectacled doctor had done nothing but take books down from the shelves, glancing through them and piling them up on the table. He was leafing through one, when, having skimmed half a page, he sat down, laughing, and said, 'Listen to this, my friends, from Diderot and Alambert's world-enlightening *Encyclopédie*, no less. It's an article on rabies. Now there are seven types of rabies: four are curable; for the rest, there is only one thing to do: *tuer le chien enragé* – kill the mad dog. And how's this for a quaint remedy: 'Take six scudi's weight of absinthe, two scudi's weight of ground aloes, two scudi's weight of roasted buckhorn, two drams of agaric, and six scudi's weight of white wine – *mêlez le tout ensemble et le faites avaler* – mix together and give to the patient to swallow.'

At this point there was a prolonged burst of laughter. But the fair-haired doctor went on unperturbed. 'Here's a medicine to prevent rabies symptoms: 'Take some milk fresh from the cow, infuse it with pimpernel. To be drunk every morning for nine days.'

His curiosity aroused by the doctors' laughter, the pharmacist had come to listen.

'Did you hear that?' he said to Gioacchino. 'Your friend simply has to drink milk with pimpernel for nine days.'

But the fourth doctor, who had not said a word so far and seemed to be dozing, got up, and taking Gioacchino aside, very solemnly whispered in his ear, 'These gentlemen may protest, but the fact is that the transmission of hydrophobia between human beings is now absolutely certain. So if the dog was rabid, your friend is past hope. The point is this: to find out whether the dog was rabid. And since rabid dogs never recover, to find out whether the dog is alive and well. If you, or your friend, or any other acquaintance of yours have need of a doctor, here is my visiting-card.'

Gioacchino left in a daze, staggering along on his thin legs, half senseless.

To find out whether the dog was alive! Gioacchino

remembered the collar he had in his pocket, and had a brilliant idea. That very same evening he went rushing to the offices of the morning newspapers, and early the following morning to the offices of the evening papers. And he placed in them the notice with which the reader has already been acquainted.

So, to return to where we left him, on the way to the bank: he arrived late, raking over in his mind countless dreadful stories of rabid dogs, and of men dying in the most frightful convulsions when they least expected it, many weeks, months, years after being bitten. Rather than go through such agony, it would be better to throw oneself into a canal straightaway, with a stone around one's neck. And he counted out the banknotes with the mechanical assurance of long habit, thinking of his poor uncle who would turn white at the sight of a dog, and sidle past, hugging the wall, and cower round corners; the same poor saintly uncle, who, having eaten bread and onions all his life, had left him one hundred thousand lire, and made him solemnly swear always to wear those knee-high boots, since dogs were in the habit of biting calves.

Zaccaria's greasy head appeared at the counter, and he said mysteriously, 'That man is here.'

'Who?'

'The one for the collar.'

Gioacchino leapt to his feet and his face lit up with joy. The owner of the collar was a tall, strong, handsome young fellow, a lieutenant in the marines, who gave the two letters asked for in the advertisement, and thanked the cashier, saying that he wanted to pay for the cost of publication, if nothing else. But Gioacchino did not reply. He was looking round, searching for the dog.

'And where's the dog?'

'The dog ran away.'

'When?'

'The day before yesterday.'

Gioacchino felt his blood run cold, and he whispered as

though talking to himself, in an agonized tone of voice, 'The day it bit Irene!'

'Exactly. He usually behaves like a lamb. But not if you pull his ears. Irene pulled them and he sank his teeth into her calf. She then gave him such a beating that he fled down the stairs, and I haven't seen him since. But he'll come back, I'm sure of it. He'll turn up at my feet either in a café or somewhere that I'm a regular visitor. It's not the first time he's played this trick on me.'

'Was the dog healthy?'

'As fit as a fiddle. But with this heat, you never know.'

Gioacchino looked up at the lieutenant's cheerful, round face and asked in a trembling voice, 'You know Irene?'

The other fellow began to laugh, as though to say, 'And who doesn't?'

'Excuse me, were you by any chance there the day before yesterday?'

'I've been going three or four times a week for the past three months, and I've taken practically all the officers in the battalion there.'

'Irene, in Calle delle Zotte, number 120? The girl who lives with her mother?'

'A fine mother she is!'

'But, you mean, Irene . . .'

'Didn't you know?'

Only then did the young man realize that the poor cashier was not feeling well, and since Gioacchino asked to be left alone, the lieutenant went away, without bothering to try to make sense of this confusion, arranging with the antiquarian from the Golden Shield for the crazy cashier to bring the collar to his house when it suited him. Zaccaria bowed so low he almost touched the ground with the two pointed tips of his grey beard.

'And she cost me one hundred lire!' Gioacchino kept repeating. And as he counted out money at his desk, his thoughts returned to the idea of tying a stone round his neck and throwing himself in a canal. Then he exclaimed,

'I want my revenge. I want to kill the old woman first of all, and then the young one.' And he trembled with fear.

At seven o'clock that evening, unaware of what he was doing, he came into the narrow street of Calle delle Zotte. The door was open. He went up and paused for a moment on the landing. He felt as though he was choking. He could not swallow his saliva any more, his hands seemed like claws, and his heart was thumping fit to burst. 'This is it,' he thought, 'I've only a few hours left to live.' And he went and stood on the threshold of Irene's room.

Irene lay stetched out on the sofa as usual, playing with a dog.

Gioacchino turned to flee, but Irene called out to him, 'Come in, come in. Look how sweet he is!'

Then talking to the dog, she said, 'You won't bite me any more, will you?'

It was the dog Gioacchino had been searching for: a healthy, lively, playful creature. Looking like a different person, Gioacchino took the collar out of his pocket and went up to the animal. Recognizing its own scent on the object, the dog jumped up at the young man, wriggling and writhing at his feet, licking his hands and dancing round him, barking with joy. Gioacchino fastened the collar round its neck. Then with one knee on the ground he stopped to stroke its soft, black, furry coat. And the dog rolled over to show its belly, waving its legs in the air.

Irene shrieked with laughter. Gioacchino suddenly stood up in a dignified manner, and trying to impart a fearsome expression to his pallid face and small, dull eyes, he said in his shrill voice, 'Madame, I leave you to the lieutenant of the marines and his battalion. I leave you to the owner of this animal. I know everything, everything . . . ' And he made resolutely for the door.

Irene's mirth was now unrestrained. She guffawed, and clapping her hands called out to the dog, 'Catch him, Buddha. Catch the thief! Catch him!' And she waved her arms at the dog.

Buddha went racing down the stairs after Gioacchino, growling, but Gioacchino was quicker and had closed the door. As he came out, the awful old woman threw down from a window the remains of a lemon on to the young man's head.

Our banker returned to his former, regular and monotonous way of life. He made no further attempts to follow pretty brunettes in the street. He started saving again, and bought a new pair of boots that also protected his knees.

THE TRANSLATOR

Christine Donougher was born in England in 1954. She read English and French at Cambridge and after a career in publishing is now a freelance translator and editor.

Her many translations from French and Italian include the Sylvie Germain novels: *The Book of Nights* and *Days of Anger*; Jan Potocki's *Tales from the Saragossa Manuscript* and Octave Mirbeau's *Le Calvaire*.

Her current projects include editing *The Dedalus Book of French Fantasy* and translating Sylvie Germain's *Nuit d'ambre*.

THE EDITOR

Roderick Conway Morris lives in Venice and writes about Italian art and culture for *The International Herald Tribune, The New York Times* and *The Spectator*.

He is the author of the novel *Jem: Memoirs of an Ottoman Secret Agent*.